A KIDNAPPING
REVIVAL

L. H. McIntosh

WestBow
PRESS
A DIVISION OF THOMAS NELSON
& ZONDERVAN

Copyright © 2020 L. H. McIntosh.

All rights reserved. No part of this book may be used or reproduced by any means, graphic, electronic, or mechanical, including photocopying, recording, taping or by any information storage retrieval system without the written permission of the author except in the case of brief quotations embodied in critical articles and reviews.

This is a work of fiction. All of the characters, names, incidents, organizations, and dialogue in this novel are either the products of the author's imagination or are used fictitiously.

WestBow Press books may be ordered through booksellers or by contacting:

WestBow Press
A Division of Thomas Nelson & Zondervan
1663 Liberty Drive
Bloomington, IN 47403
www.westbowpress.com
844-714-3454

Because of the dynamic nature of the Internet, any web addresses or links contained in this book may have changed since publication and may no longer be valid. The views expressed in this work are solely those of the author and do not necessarily reflect the views of the publisher, and the publisher hereby disclaims any responsibility for them.

Any people depicted in stock imagery provided by Getty Images are models, and such images are being used for illustrative purposes only. Certain stock imagery © Getty Images.

Scripture taken from the New King James Version®. Copyright © 1982 by Thomas Nelson. Used by permission. All rights reserved.

ISBN: 978-1-9736-9806-7 (sc)
ISBN: 978-1-9736-9807-4 (hc)
ISBN: 978-1-9736-9805-0 (e)

Library of Congress Control Number: 2020913087

Print information available on the last page.

WestBow Press rev. date: 08/14/2020

CHAPTER 1

Riley runs from his house, barely able to get his feet to work, so all-consuming is his fear. His chest is heaving; he feels like he is moving slowly; he runs for his life.

The mile is long and winding. He cannot see his destination. And he dares not look back.

After what seems like hours, Riley sees Uncle Gary's home, a brownstone house, set back from the forest trail. Though the house is dark, bugs are flying around the porch light like they always do.

He knocks.

Nothing.

So, he knocks harder.

Finally, Uncle Gary, in his pajamas and holding a shotgun, opens the door. When he looks out, he does not see anything, but when he looks down, he puts the gun aside and pulls Riley into the house.

Reaching down to pick up the boy, he asks, "What happened, son?"

It is late. Anna sends her only child to his uncle's house as soon as she hears someone coming down the long driveway. She followed this routine once before and knows he is safe.

A gunshot shatters the silence and her nerves. She gathers what little strength she has, but before she can take a breath, she sees a human form materialize outside. The stranger looks at her. She feels like a mannequin in a store window. He carries an aluminum bat.

Where is her cell phone? She runs to the bedroom to find her phone and her husband's gun, though she does not know if she can pull the trigger. She finds neither. She remembers he probably left his gun in the kitchen after cleaning it. The cell phone is nowhere. As she rushes to the kitchen, the front door is splintered, and two men burst in. She runs toward the back patio, but one of the men grabs her.

In the few seconds she sees the intruders, one looks like he has been wearing the same clothes for a while: dirty, washed-out jeans, a t-shirt that has the name of some baseball team and a few stains on it, a bandanna, longish hair, and a beard.

The other guy is clean-shaven and somewhat well dressed, with a pronounced limp and dark eyes. He points a pistol at her. She does not move.

The bearded man leers at her and pushes her down on the couch with a nasty laugh. He handcuffs her, binds her feet, and blindfolds her. He then hoists her up and throws her into the cargo hold of what she thinks is a large SUV. She is having muscle spasms. She starts taking deep breaths, and when she reins in her emotions for a nanosecond, she silently thanks God she sent Riley away. He must have made it safely, as he had been there often. Gary and Beth had no children, and they would care for Riley with all their hearts.

Anna tries not to consider the possibilities for her future. She senses the cargo space is large and empty, and she shivers, for it is cold, and she has never been so frightened in her life. She knows God will never leave or forsake her, and she can run to him whenever she is afraid. She holds on to her hope in God with every breath, and his palpable presence in the cargo hold reassures her. She seesaws between faith and fear until utterly exhausted, and she falls into a troubled sleep.

When she wakes up, the vehicle is still moving. Since she has no idea how long she slept, she has no idea how far they have traveled. She wonders where her cell phone is. She does not know the time; she cannot see where they are; and she cannot guess where they are headed.

When questioned by his uncle Gary, there is no answer other than crying. Gary strokes Riley's back and cradles his head. Once he calms slightly, he says, "Uncle Gary, I was so scared."

Gary said, "Tell me what happened."

Beth quietly enters the room.

"Daddy's not home, and Momma told me if somebody we didn't know was coming, to run and not turn around until I got here. So tonight, somebody came; Momma told me to run; and I did."

"Did you see who came?"

"No. I'm sorry, Uncle Gary. I did not look back. Momma told me not to," Riley said as he broke into tears again.

"It's okay, son. You did what you were supposed to do. Your daddy will be proud of you, and your momma will be too. Aunt Beth will fix you a special treat, and I will go over to your house and check on everything. Do not wait up for me. You know it takes me longer to look at things than other people because I am a policeman. I'll see you in the morning."

"Come here, Riley, you sweet boy," Beth says as she tenderly wraps him in a hug. "You come with Aunt Beth to the kitchen, and we'll have ourselves some hot chocolate. I think we might find one of your favorite cookies."

Gary rushes to Alan and Anna's home, thinking of the courage it took for Riley to run that distance in the middle of the night. Gary approaches the house, a country home with a big front porch, reached by a long driveway with only one neighbor. Anna's car is there, but Alan's truck is at the Memphis airport.

He calls out to Anna, hoping for an answer. There is none. A look in all the rooms and closets and all around the house, including the root cellar and shed, reveals nothing missing except Anna. It is a kidnapping, not a burglary. The time, 3:15 a.m. The date, May 10, 2004. The place, northeast Mississippi.

As a police detective, Gary knows the evidence will depend primarily on the experience and skill of the kidnappers. It is unlikely anyone saw a strange vehicle, but he will check with the neighbor in a few hours. For now, he calls Billy Blue, the closest thing the department has to a crime scene investigator. Billy is as round as Gary is lean, and his hair is bright red. Most of the force call him "Red."

Billy came right away, and as he steps up onto the front porch, he says, "It wasn't like I was sleeping or nothing. Ain't this your brother's place? The one who is a preacher?"

"Yes. I know it is early, but this *is* my brother we are talking about. His little seven-year-old boy ran all the way to my house."

As they walk into the house, Billy says, "Looks like somebody done used a tire iron or metal bar to break down the door. It may be 'round here. There was a struggle, and there's a cell phone."

"Yes, I think it belongs to Anna," said Gary, as he picks it up. "It does, because the last call she made was to the hotel where Alan is staying in Atlanta. Alan gave me the number too."

"Well, Gary, I don't see no footprints, but I'll dust for them as well as fingerprints. It will take me no time at all."

"What's your take on this?" asked Billy. "Has Brother Alan got a lot of money? Miss Anna? Have they done somebody wrong? Do you think Miss Anna done run away and just made it seem like she was kidnapped? Or do you reckon Brother Alan done had her kidnapped?"

"No," Gary said. "Alan is a preacher, and Anna is a nurse, so unless one of them has a gambling addiction or sells drugs on the side, which is about as likely as a snowstorm in Miami, money is not be the motive."

Gary looked around the house and added, "On the other hand, revenge might be. You know how some people hate Christians. If Alan offended the wrong person with his preaching—well, it is a stretch, but it could be the motive."

He scratches his head. "As to the idea Anna staged the kidnapping, she loves Alan and Riley too much. You can see their love for each other whenever you're around them." He stretches his arms wide and said, "Unless I'm a total fool, she would never put Alan and Riley through this. The same goes for Alan. He is head over heels in love with Anna, and little Riley means the world to him. There's no way he had her kidnapped."

"How 'bout one of them cheated somebody in some business deal gone bad?"

"It's nothing like that. It bothers me, though, how they knew Alan would be gone tonight."

When Gary gets back home, Beth is waiting for him. Riley had calmed down after having something to eat, and Beth had rocked him to sleep. Gary says, "Anna has been kidnapped."

"Oh, no, how will we tell Riley—and Alan?"

He tries to call Alan, who is in Atlanta, on the hotel phone.

No answer. He tries his cell phone. No answer. The call goes to voicemail, and Gary leaves a message for him to call him back immediately.

They have an early breakfast at the kitchen bar. Riley sleeps in the small room they prepared for the child they never had. They talk about what to do. Are they at risk? Is this a grudge or payback for something the parents had done or left undone? Could his brother and his wife be into something dangerous?

There is much he does not know, but one thing he does: He wants his family and Riley to be safe, so they need to do what his parents did when things got out of control. They established a compound, their safe place when the world became too much for them. His father was a research scientist co-opted at times by the federal government to work on highly classified projects. He worked at the compound when there was too much going on in Washington, and they spent most of their holidays at the compound. It is in Tishomingo County, the backwoods of northeast Mississippi, and is surrounded by creeks, swamps, and forests with plentiful wildlife. It has several buildings enclosed by a wall and protected by the latest technology. The security has never been breached.

As they drive into the compound. Riley's eyes get big when he sees houses inside what looks like a park. A big iron gate stands before them. Gary punches in some numbers, and a voice requests information. After a few minutes of back and forth, they roll into the enclosure.

Beth said, "Are you sure, Gary, about leaving our home?"

Gary said, "Yes, hon. I want you and Riley to be safe. Plus, I think you will like it here. It doesn't have to be permanent."

"It seems so remote."

"That's the beauty of it. Safety and security in a beautiful, natural environment. You'll get adjusted to it, and you probably won't want to leave!"

At the time Gary called, Alan was asleep. When he finally awakens, he is late, so he does not check his phone. Instead, he grabs his Bible and his laptop and rushes to the Atlanta hotel ballroom for his presentation.

The room holds about a hundred chairs, and they are almost filled.

Alan says, "To start this discussion, consider the numbers from Voice of the Martyrs. About 75 percent of all religious intolerance is directed at Christianity. More than three hundred Christians are killed every month for their faith; over one hundred churches and other Christian buildings are burned or attacked each month; and over two hundred Christians are arrested, sentenced, or imprisoned each month. One out of nine Christians experiences persecution.

"Just think about those numbers for a minute. Over three hundred Christians killed each month just because they are Christians. Persecution is coming to America and has, in fact, already started here. We let them take prayer out of our schools. We will talk more about that in a few minutes.

"The main thing to take back to your congregations is to stand strong and not give in to panic and fear. Jesus said, 'Love your enemies, bless those who curse you, do good to those who hate you, and pray for those who spitefully use you and persecute you.' That is found in Matthew, chapter five, verse forty-four, and in the other gospels as well. This is to be the response to our persecutors: Love them, bless them, do good for them, and pray for them. Luke goes even further and tells us to rejoice when we are persecuted. That scripture is from Luke, chapter six, verse twenty-three."

After about forty-five minutes, Charles Winters, chairman of the conference, announces a break. Alan checks his phone. After he listens to Gary's voicemail, he steps outside the hotel to call him back. For Gary to have called him so early in the morning, it must be serious.

Hearing about the kidnapping takes Alan's breath away, but he manages to say, "Thank God, Riley is safe, but oh no—please, God, not my Anna. Do you know who or what or why? Oh, God, please protect Anna wherever she is, God, and please, please bring her back to me!"

"Alan, we won't stop investigating until we find her. Billy has already checked out the house, and we have moved to the compound for safety."

As soon as Alan gets off the phone, he goes to Charles and tells him what had happened. It is all he can do to remain calm. Charles said, "Go home. I will tell the conference why you left. You and Anna will be covered in prayer."

Alan goes to the front desk to ask them to check flights for him to Memphis. He books one and goes to his room to pack. As he finishes packing, there is a knock. Standing at the door is a young man who hands him an envelope. He takes it, turns around and rips it open, crying out when he reads the words: "I have Anna."

CHAPTER 2

Anna calculates her possibility of escape as the vehicle slows. She cannot open the back doors with her hands and feet bound. For the same reason, any hope of knocking one of them out is a dumb thought. She cannot even see. Maybe she can talk her way out of the situation.

"Hello, is anyone listening?" Anna asks.

"No, shut up!"

Undaunted, Anna asks, "Where are you taking me?"

"If you don't shut up, the only place you will be going is into the ground."

Anna says nothing after the last retort. When the vehicle stops, the men get out, leaving her in the vehicle. She hears metal slam into concrete when the door closes. She needs the bathroom, and she is incredibly thirsty. No one comes to the garage to check on her. She thinks, *What kind of kidnapper forgets his victim?*

After a while, the back doors open, and a man reaches in, pulls her out, and undoes the binding around her hands and feet. He leads her into the house, guiding her up the stairs, as she is still blindfolded. To have held a gun on her at her home, the man now seems calm and gentle. She removes her blindfold in the windowless bathroom.

When she comes out, she sees the men left while she was in the bathroom, and she finds herself in the custody of a woman, who is pretty and seems to be about Anna's age. Armed with a .38, she looks capable and eager to use it. Anna tries to start a conversation with no success, except learning the woman's name, Mrs. Bosco. She sends Anna to a bedroom, with adjoining bathroom and no windows, and locks her in.

"Thank you, Lord Jesus," Anna prays, "for keeping me safe this far. I pray for Alan and all my family, especially little Riley. I ask you to use me to reach Mrs. Bosco for you. I love you, Lord. You are my hiding place." Feeling emotionally exhausted, she goes to sleep when her head hits the pillow.

At the Atlanta airport, Alan rushes to the gate and waits for what seems like a long time before he boards the plane. Panic keeps threatening to erupt. His seat mate, a man about his age, wants to talk, the last thing Alan wants to do. He listens politely and makes appropriate sounds, asking God to forgive him for his attitude. As the plane lands in Memphis, Alan wonders how he can cope.

Thinking someone might be waiting for him, Alan decides to reconnoiter. He approaches the parking garage quietly and sees a man in a silver suburban looking at his truck. Waiting for a passenger, perhaps, but his interest in Alan's truck seems strange.

Alan runs through his options—hop into his truck and leave, confident the watcher will follow him, or sneak up behind the man and get his vehicle and license plate information. Choosing the second option, Alan tries to stay out of sight as he uses his phone to photograph the vehicle and license plate.

He sends the photographs to Gary, along with the message, "If I don't show up at the compound tonight, look for a man in this vehicle."

Gary texted back, "Stay put. I will grab Honcho. It will take us a couple of hours, so if your guy gets antsy, let us know, and we will change the plan. No heroics on your part, little brother. They don't end well, as I remember."

Alan gives him the parking garage information and sits with his back against a pillar away from the watcher but where he can still see him. He thinks about Riley and how much he loves him. Trying to take the guy on his own would be stupid; being a father to his son keeps him going.

Gary's comment about heroics made Alan remember when he was about Riley's age, one of his friends fell into a hole. There was no water in the hole, but the walls were too steep for the boy to climb out. Alan put a board over the edges of the hole to get him out. When Alan stepped on the board, the end jerked up, so he fell on top of Randy. He broke his arm and hurt Randy's leg. If Alan had not been hurt, he would have been punished. Instead, his father gave him a tongue lashing for not being more careful and not asking for help.

Alan continues to lean against the cold pillar and sit on the hard cement. He thinks about another tongue lashing given to him by his father, this time after he dropped out of college. His father did not understand Alan's unrelenting need to drink, nor did he try. After three months of mutual misery, during which Alan continued to drink, notwithstanding his efforts not to, he was given a tongue lashing and ultimatum by his father: If he did not enter an inpatient rehabilitation facility, he would kick him out and bar him from ever returning to the Livingston home.

Gary and Honcho park on the floor below. With drawn pistols, they approach the man who has let his window down to smoke. The man whirls around, dropping his cigarette into his lap, and reaching for his firearm. Gary and Honcho easily take him down, handcuff him, and load him into their vehicle. Gary takes the prisoner, and Honcho drives the man's suburban.

On the way home, Alan's fear for Anna grows so intense, he must pull to the side of the road. He cannot drive; he can only cry and scream at God. Alan knows God is in control, but his life is over if Anna does not return. Weeping until he can weep no more, he heads home.

Memories flood his mind, and he breaks down again as he looks around the house where he and Anna and Riley lived, now showing signs of violence. He wishes he had never gone to the conference, thinking maybe he could have prevented the kidnapping. Trying to concentrate, he gets everything packed and heads to the compound.

He has good memories of the compound too, he thinks as he drives, memories of his dad and mom and Gary. They spent many summers and holidays there, fishing and hunting and digging up arrowheads. Horses and cats and dogs lived together in the barn, not always peacefully.

Manny and Esther Torres stayed at the compound year-round and kept the grounds and buildings ready for occupancy. Esther took care of Gary and Alan when they were young. The couple stayed on after the parents died. The horses were sold, but they still had dogs and a few cats. They had no children. Gary and Alan called them aunt and uncle, and Alan knew they would love Riley.

"Daddy, Daddy, you're here! Aunt Beth made me cookies, and I helped Uncle Manny wash the deck, and Princess has puppies. Aunt Esther let me hold one. Daddy, I want to show you the puppies, and then will you read me a book?"

A KIDNAPPING REVIVAL

"Hold up, partner! I cannot keep up with you! I have not even seen Uncle Manny or Aunt Esther yet. The puppies will have to wait. I love you, Riley Meyer Livingston, and I am so proud of you. Uncle Gary told me how you ran all the way from our house last night. You are a brave boy."

The man they apprehended at the airport is Larry Reed. Gary explains to him his position as a police detective, working in a semiprivate capacity, because of the kidnapping of his sister-in-law.

"My partner, a retired police detective, works for the Livingston family," Gary said. "If you do not cooperate, we will not hesitate to take you to the police station and charge you with kidnapping. So, you have a choice. You can cooperate with us or take your chances at the police station. It is up to you. Which do you choose?"

"I'd rather not go to the police station. How can I cooperate with you?"

"Answer our questions completely and truthfully."

Questioning Larry lasts several hours. They interview him in the security office of the compound. Gary and Larry sit across from each other at the table. Larry is still handcuffed, and Honcho stands at the door.

"Why were you watching Alan?" asked Gary.

"Because the boss told me to."

"What else were you supposed to do?"

"That was it. I knew they had kidnapped a preacher's wife, and I was supposed to watch the preacher and report to the boss."

"Where is she?"

"I don't know."

"Who is the boss?"

"I don't know his name, and I have never met him."

"Who else is involved in the kidnapping?"

"I don't know."

The interview continues, and the questions cover Larry's entire life. It turns out that Honcho knows Larry's father, whom Larry has not seen for years. Gary and Honcho decide to keep Larry for a few days to see what they can get out of him. They believe he knows more than he said.

The next morning, Alan goes to see Anna's dad, Jon Meyer, at his home, an hour away. Jon had worked as an accountant for most of his life. He retired, and his wife died of cancer just one year later. Jon mourns his wife's death, which affects him physically, mentally, and spiritually, and he is completely incapable of processing his daughter's kidnapping.

Alan stays longer than he intends and gives Jon's pastor, Brother Joe Miller, a call after he leaves to tell him about Anna's kidnapping and Jon's difficulties. Brother Joe says he prays and visits Jon often. He tells Alan he will pray for Anna, check on Jon regularly, and help him in any way.

Anna stays in her bed, leaning against the headboard. Though Mrs. Bosco continues to keep her weapon at the ready, she has made no threats. Being kidnapped and Mrs. Bosco's involvement in the crime remain upmost in Anna's mind. Still, she needs to get along with her captor. She makes herself join her. Mrs. Bosco stops cooking and grabs her weapon off the counter.

Anna, raising her hands, says, "Mrs. Bosco, I have no intention of trying to escape; I don't want to die. You treat me well. I like you."

Mrs. Bosco's mouth twitches at the corner, which to Anna looks like an attempt to smile. Mrs. Bosco says a few words, but Anna believes they are prayers. She begins to pray for Mrs.

Bosco, who slips her gun into her apron pocket. Anna thinks of tackling her but gives up the idea when she realizes she told Mrs. Bosco she would not try to escape. And there is the likelihood she would be shot.

Anna thinks back to a conversation she heard between her abductors. The one she thought of as the leader said, "I have never been treated so bad in my life as a preacher treated me."

The other man said, "The fewer Christians in the world, the better the world will be."

The leader then told the other man about her status as a preacher's wife. He added that her husband was *that* preacher, whatever that meant. She remembers everything, though remembering makes her physically ill.

She wonders about the attitudes of these two men. Were they anti-Christian, or did they hate preachers, one preacher in particular—her husband? In either case, did Alan's role as a Christian preacher cause her kidnapping?

Anna ponders another comment made by one of the kidnappers who said he wished he knew whether the kidnapping would be the end of it. *The end of what?*

CHAPTER 3

After a few days, Larry begins to show subtle signs of softening. Riley has taken to Larry in a way that touches Larry's heart. The adults have shown him love too. Still, he sticks to his testimony.

"Larry," Alan said, "I have shown considerable restraint with you, considering my wife's life is at stake, and I believe you can help us find her. It takes everything in me and God's grace to keep me from trying to beat answers out of you. Think about this. You may make all the money in the world; or you may spend your life in prison; you may tell me everything; or you may tell me nothing. But whatever you own, whatever happens to you, whatever you do, without Jesus Christ, your future is doomed. Only Jesus can take your life and make it mean something and then guarantee you a future and a hope of heaven. Think about that long and hard. It's not just Anna's life; your eternal life is also at stake."

After the confrontation with Larry, Alan wants nothing more than to go to sleep, but he has not eaten or showered or shaved or seen his son since the night before. He wants Anna. She is part of him; he of her; the two of them one. And one missing half of itself does not function.

"Oh, God, please help Anna; help me. Please help Riley and touch Larry's heart. But most of all, dear Lord, your will be done in all our lives and in all situations facing us. I trust you, worship you, love you. In Jesus's name, amen."

After praying, Alan looks in on sleeping Riley, and then he falls asleep as he drops onto the bed. Everything else can wait for another day.

Larry tosses and turns as he considers Alan's words. He has never really looked at life like that but finds he wants to believe. He thinks about his past, having spent so much time locked up as a teenager and living on the edge as an adult. At this rate, he will end up dead or in prison. And if he dies, he will go to hell. He needs to do something now, tonight. Since he does not know what or how, he asks God about it.

"God, if you're there and if you want me to believe, you'll have to help me. You know I have not lived a good life, and I should not ask, but if you will have me, I want to believe in you. Please forgive me, and please help me, Jesus. Amen."

Larry hopes he asked right. For the first time in years, he thinks about his father, who Honcho said lives nearby, and his sister. He finds himself wanting to see them. Surprised at the direction his thoughts take him, he wonders if the Lord put those thoughts in his mind as he drifts off to sleep.

Billy gets back to Gary on the forensic evidence from Alan's home and the suburban driven from the airport by Honcho. No useable prints or other evidence was found. The suburban, however, is registered to Dillon Dubois, an attorney. Mr. Dubois says he has no information on the vehicle other than it is no longer in the garage in his law firm's building.

The lack of forensic evidence makes Larry's testimony important. Alan wants to question Larry aggressively, but he decides to back off and let the Lord work. He has learned through the years not to press people too hard, but to follow the leading of the Holy Spirit.

Alan has not returned to the church since coming back from Atlanta. The visiting pastor, Joshua Strange, who covered for Alan while he was at the conference, stays for one more Sunday. Alan hopes he feels like preaching by the next Sunday. Right now, he feels like punching someone.

Anna says, "Mrs. Bosco, may I ask who pays you to guard me? And why do you do it? I mean, you are an accessory to kidnapping, and you face prison as a result. Aren't you concerned?"

"Mrs. Livingston, you don't know what you ask. I cannot discuss my boss, but I assure you he will not allow me to go to prison. You shouldn't ask me these things."

Anna does not know how to respond to Mrs. Bosco. Unnerved, she abandons her questioning and withdraws to her bedroom.

Alan and Riley walk to a creek on the property to do some serious fishing. One of the puppies follows them. Not long after they arrive, Alan gets a message from Gary. Alan calls him back and invites him to join them.

About that time, both bobbins sink. Alan grabs the poles before they go downstream. Riley jumps up and down; the puppy runs in circles; and Alan, with a big smile, holds up the lines to show Riley the two catfish.

"Uncle Gary," said Riley, "come see what I caught. Can you fish with us?"

"Yes, sir, if you have enough bait and you don't mind a little competition."

"What's competition?"

"It means I try to catch more fish or a bigger fish than you do."

"I bet I can catch a bigger fish than you can, Uncle Gary!"

"We'll see about that, young man!"

"Gary," Alan said, "what did you need to see me about?"

"Larry wants to talk with you, Alan. I can fish with Riley."

"Thanks, Gary. You two leave me some fish."

Alan finds Larry waiting for him in the library. He says, "Larry, you want to see me?" Larry jumps up from his chair and stands until Alan motions for him to sit. Alan sits across from him.

"Yes, Mr. Livingston. I prayed to Jesus. He has given me a new way to think about things. I'm going to answer your questions no matter what."

Alan listens with skepticism, as he knows some criminals pretend to find Jesus to curry favor.

"Larry, everyone will be thrilled you have made Jesus your Lord and Savior. I am excited you are willing to answer questions. But how am I supposed to know if you are telling me the truth?"

"I promise I won't lie to you."

"Okay, fair enough. I will ask you a few questions.

"Were you involved in the kidnapping?"

"I was not involved, but I knew about it."

"How did you know about it?"

"They hired me to keep an eye on you because of the kidnapping."

Alan purses his lips, shifts his weight, and asks, "Who hired you?"

"The kidnappers."

Alan is getting weary of having to pull the answers from Larry but plows on.

"Who were the kidnappers?"

"Roger Cutlow and Jim Boren."

Alan is surprised Larry named the kidnappers. "Do you know where we can find Roger and Jim?"

"No."

This answer is not a surprise to Alan, who asks then, "Why did they kidnap Anna?"

"I'm not sure. The only thing they talked about was you. They want to hurt you, and they don't like preachers."

Alan flinches like he has been punched and asks, "What did I do to them?"

"I don't know. They hate all preachers, but they hate you the most."

"Is there anything else you can tell me?"

"Yes, I think Roger and Jim work for somebody else, and I don't think they plan to hurt your wife."

Alan rises from his chair, trying to decide whether to believe Larry, and asks, "What do they plan to do with her?"

"I don't know."

After struggling with the lack of information, Alan reaches out his hand to Larry and says, "Thank you, Larry. I appreciate your answering my questions. Congratulations on your decision to follow Jesus. I've got a Bible for you."

Almost as soon as they finish, Gary and Riley show up with a big string of fish. "Wow, Riley, how did you catch so many fish?"

"Uncle Gary helped me, and I beat him in the competition."

"Great! We will take these fish to Aunt Beth. Maybe she and Aunt Esther will want to cook them tonight. You need to get your bath, and I bet you're hungry."

"Gary, Larry answered some questions for me," Alan said.

Gary said, "Come on, Larry. We will go to the security office, and you can answer some more questions for me."

A KIDNAPPING REVIVAL

Alan turns the pages of his Bible, his first time back in his office since the kidnapping. It is a good distance from the compound, but he needs to be alone with God, with his focus on him alone. His secretary, Corinne, stays in her area; she knows not to disturb him when she sees his closed door.

Alan's mind wanders, yet he finds himself studying God's presence. The crowd was "with one accord" when God appeared, as reported in the first verse of the second chapter of Acts. He wonders if his congregation is with one accord in their devotion for the Lord to appear to them.

As Alan digs into the Word of God, Gary calls.

Gary says, "Alan, maybe our parents did something to trigger this crime."

"Like what?"

"We know so little about what Dad did. Maybe the kidnapping relates to his work, like someone taking revenge against us for whatever he said or did. It's something to consider."

"We can talk when I get back to the compound. Is Beth cooking those fish we caught yesterday, or should I pick up something for dinner?"

"She and Aunt Esther are cooking; Riley is with Manny in the garden; and Honcho is watching over everyone. By the way, Larry got a job as a janitor and lives in an apartment in the building where he works. He gave me his address."

Later, Alan sits down across from Gary at the compound, and says, "I just can't imagine Mom or Dad would have incited such long-lasting hatred or other reason for the kidnapping. Do you really think that's a possibility?"

"I don't know. Dad was so secretive about his work. My imagination runs wild," says Gary. "If nothing else looks like the motivation, then we check out the family connection," Gary said as he walked around the library, looking at the portraits of their ancestors.

Alan said, "That sounds like the mafia!"

"What about Christian persecution, Alan—that your wife was kidnapped to punish you for being a Christian pastor?"

"I don't know, but if someone hated Christianity enough, they might want to hurt me because I am a pastor." Alan straightened books on the shelves.

"Alan, I hate to ask, but do you have a side interest that would cause someone to take such a drastic step? Do you gamble or do drugs?"

Alan whirled around and said loudly, "You are kidding, aren't you? I cannot believe you would ask me such a thing. How dare you accuse me?"

"I'm not accusing you, but I still had to ask," said Gary. "Forget I said anything."

Alan slams the door as he leaves. As he thinks later about personal enemies, however, his anger fades, and fear creeps in.

CHAPTER 4

A week and a half later, Alan holds Sunday services for the first time since Anna was kidnapped.

"Good morning. Let us go to our God in prayer. Father God, we thank you this morning for all your many blessings. We give you praise, for you deserve all the honor and glory. We ask for forgiveness for our sins and you to bring this country, as well as each of us, back to you. We lift Anna up to you and ask you to protect her and give her peace. We pray for others taken like Anna was and all who are suffering. Lord, we ask you to bring back Anna and those who have lost their way. We also pray for Anna's kidnappers. We pray for the peace of Jerusalem. We pray for your presence to be with us this morning and in our lives. Above all, we pray your will be done. In the mighty name of Jesus. Amen.

"We do not know where Anna is, but we know the one who does. And he is still on the throne. Now turn with—"

Before Alan can go on, he is interrupted by a man who walks down the middle aisle of the church like he owns the place and addresses the congregation: "Mrs. Livingston was kidnapped because she is a Christian. All of you face the same danger as long as you attend this church and call yourselves Christians."

"Excuse me, Mr.—"

"Jason Stone is my name. I've been sent here by God to warn

you they may kidnap you; they may put you in jail or prison; they may take everything you own; and they may kill you if you don't turn your back on Jesus and quit hanging on to your religion. You'd better stop coming to this church if you do not want these bad things to happen to you. This is the only warning you will get."

"We have questions, Mr. Stone."

"I don't answer questions," Stone says as he exits the sanctuary.

The congregation talks hysterically until Alan catches his breath and says loudly, "God will answer our questions." He stops for a few moments to let that sink in and to let everyone stop talking. "Do not focus on Jason Stone, but see what God's Word has to say about persecution. In the tenth chapter of Matthew, Jesus clearly explains we, as Christians, will be persecuted because he was persecuted, and we are his followers. He counsels us not to be afraid. But how can we not be afraid? In the tenth chapter of Mark, verse twenty-seven, Jesus says that 'with men, it is impossible, but not with God, for with God, all things are possible.' Remember, the battle belongs to the Lord. It is all about him.

"Knowing these verses is a good beginning, but we must do more. We must believe. We must believe God. God is not surprised Jason Stone interrupted our service today. And he is not surprised by what you are thinking at this very moment. He loves you. He will never leave you nor forsake you.

"If anyone this morning has not given his life to Jesus, come forward during the altar call, and I will pray with you, or pray where you are. Just make sure you do this now. This is the most important decision of your life. For those who have made Jesus their Savior but still feel fear and worry, come to the altar, and leave your fears at the feet of Jesus. He will walk you through any darkness. Nothing is too hard for him."

As the music continues, several come forward, and some pray to accept Jesus as their Lord and Savior. Alan introduces them to the congregation and asks everyone to stay after service and welcome them into the body of Christ.

"Pray for strength and courage. Remember to pray for Anna, for each other, the church, the lost, and for Mr. Stone."

Alan dismisses the congregation, thanking God for the service. As Alan greets the congregation individually, he notices some do not look him in the eye but look down and around. They do not say much, whereas they usually cannot wait to tell him all about their families.

"Hello, Dad," said Larry. "Do you know who I am?"

"Well, only two people in the world would call me dad, and one is a girl. I guess that makes you my son, Larry."

"You're right. Would you have known me if I hadn't called you dad?"

"Probably not. It's been how long, twelve years?"

"No, only about ten. I have changed a lot since I was seventeen, but you have not changed much. I want to ask you to forgive me for getting in so much trouble and leaving home the way I did."

"You don't sound much like the Larry I knew, but you've got to go now. It is my nap time. Come again if you want."

"Sure. See you later," Larry said. He contemplates whether he will return to see his old man, who sounds as sullen as always. Will God require more than just forgiveness from Larry? He knows the answer to that as soon as the question enters his mind. Forgiveness invites action. For Larry to forgive his father but leave him without Jesus is not true forgiveness. God would not be pleased, and Larry would feel guilty.

Anna is depressed. She is kept in a small house, with white walls and no attempt at decorating, looking like the construction crew just left. Her bedroom contains a bed and nightstand and nothing else. Her tiny bathroom has no vanity and only a small shower.

Anna wonders if anyone has a clue as to where to find her. She does not know where she is. She dreams about Alan rescuing her, coming in through an imaginary window and kissing her until she awakens. Acutely disappointed when she wakes up, she throws her pillow across the room and breaks down sobbing. She prays for Alan and for their son and for her dad. She also prays for Mrs. Bosco.

"Mrs. Bosco," said Anna, "I'd like a pen and paper to write letters to my family. Do you know what's going to happen to me?"

"I'll get you a pen and paper when I send for groceries after a while. I don't know your future, Anna, but I think you will find out before too much longer."

"Good or bad?"

"I don't know."

Anna fights back tears, returns to her room, and silently cries out to God.

Alan tasks Corinne with calling all Good News members to find out if they need anything, and if they intend to return to the church. She finds some have plans to attend future services; some do not answer repeated calls; and some hang up. Some talk about their many responsibilities, their health, their families, anything but the incident at Sunday's service. Corinne encourages everyone, inviting them to the compound for a special devotional service.

"The newly saved adults all responded enthusiastically," said Corinne to Alan.

He said, "God is in control and will deliver the people from their fear and bring revival."

CHAPTER 5

Forty-seven adults show up at the compound devotional service. One of the members brings his little boy to play with Riley, and Beth entertains them. Alan is fighting depression, so he speaks on joy.

"The joy of the Lord is my strength. Even in our darkest hours, we must know the Lord of the universe is personally concerned with us. He is moving heaven and earth to address our needs. Hold on to God, my friends, and let his joy reign in the deepest recesses of your heart. In fact, Jesus tells us in the sixth chapter of Luke to rejoice and 'leap for joy' when men hate us because we love him."

Alan's phone rings.

"Fire! Fire! My house is on fire!" Alan races from the compound and speeds toward his home. Blue lights shine, and a siren sounds behind him, but he goes even faster to get there. When he arrives, the policemen jump out of their cruiser ready to arrest him but hold back when they realize the house being consumed by the raging fire belongs to him.

Thankful none of the family was home and the fire destroyed only temporary things, Alan still feels great sorrow deep in his soul, so overpowering he can barely stand. He turns away from the fire.

"Alan, over here," said Honcho.

For a long moment, Alan stands still and says nothing. Then he finds his voice and joins Honcho, standing against a fire truck. "Honcho, how much more can I take! God promises all things work together for good, even including a kidnapping, a crazy man's threats, and a house burning—because the Bible says 'all' things. But he did not say how long working together will take. How long, Honcho?"

"Beats me, Alan, but you know God keeps his promises."

"Honcho, it's not that I don't know, but knowing is not enough. Something has got to change! I cannot take any more! Why is God letting this happen to me? I know I'm a sinner, but how can I ever preach when I feel so let down by God?"

"I can't imagine what you're going through, Alan, but I will help you any way I can. Over there is the fire chief. Why don't we go over and see what he has to say?"

"Hello, I'm Harry Woods. We got here as soon as we could, given the confusion, but we only saved the car shed. The car inside should be okay. Was there anything left on in the house, like the stove, an iron, anything like that?"

"No. I checked everything last night. There was nothing left on. I'm sure about that."

"Well, we'll have our investigator come take a look and let you know what we find. I sure am sorry about your loss."

"What did you mean earlier when you said confusion?"

"Someone called the fire in, and then someone called and said there was no fire. We came anyway in case the first call was correct."

"What? Why would there be confusion? If a fire is called in, you act, no matter what anybody says about it. There shouldn't be any confusion about that!" Alan said and then turns away taking one last look.

A KIDNAPPING REVIVAL

Larry leaves the Sunset after visiting his father, and he spots his old partner and nemesis, Jim Boren, parked across the street. Larry goes to his car. *Why is he here? Is the boss upset with me for getting caught?* He considers driving away, but he needs to face him. Jim always taunted Larry, though he never hurt him when Roger was around.

Larry gets three numbers off Jim's tag as he drives away and stops at a diner in case Jim wants to talk. At least the meeting will be in a public place. When he sees Jim is still in his car, he enters the diner and orders coffee. Then he sends the three numbers, vehicle description, Jim's name and what he did, and location to Gary. Staying put to give Gary time to get there, Larry has another cup of coffee and a stale doughnut and prays for Gary to arrive soon.

An unmarked car drives up to the nearly deserted diner and parks behind Jim. Gary and another plainclothes officer get out and draw their firearms. Jim makes no move; Gary handcuffs him; and hands him off to a uniformed policeman, who drives up. Gary then goes inside the diner and says, "Thank you, Larry. I appreciate your letting me know he was here."

"Well, seeing him made me nervous since I abandoned my job of following Alan. Jim could have turned me in to the kidnapping boss."

Alan calls his home insurance carrier to report his claim on the house fire and is told his coverage lapsed due to nonpayment of the last premium.

"What do you mean you haven't received the payment? When was the due date? My wife pays our bills, and she never misses a payment. You'd better double-check your files. You're wrong!" Alan says as he slams down the phone.

Anna is always current, so maybe the bill became due after she was kidnapped. He will check, he thinks, and then he remembers most of the records burned along with the house. He hangs his head in defeat.

The next morning, Alan gets a call before he puts his feet on the floor. He grimaces when he sees who it is. He has enough to focus on, but said, "Charles, this is a surprise. I hadn't expected to hear from you."

"Well, I called to see how I can help. I am so sorry about the house fire on top of Anna's kidnapping. Almost too much for a man to handle, but we serve an awesome God, Alan, and he instructs us to help one another, to be his hands and feet on the earth. A group of pastors from the conference and I want to offer our resources to you."

Alan manages to navigate the room in search of his robe, and as Charles talks, he tries to find some coffee.

"Charles, how did you hear about the house fire?"

"The district office called me. I think they may want me to preach for you if you need me to."

"Thanks for the offer. I am managing. I do not know if you heard about this, but our church service this past Sunday was interrupted by a strange man who tried to scare the congregation. He said persecution is coming, which is usually my message. His remarks, however, created fear, and many of the congregation probably will not return to church."

"Alan, I did hear about someone advising people to go undercover to avoid persecution. What's this man's name?"

By this time, Alan feels exhausted by the conversation. *Why does Charles pay me so much attention? How does he know so much? Why does he think I want him to preach in my place? Who is he?*

Alan calls Nathan Horowitz, a lawyer he met at the conference. Nathan led a discussion advising pastors on legal matters from a Christian viewpoint.

"Good morning, Pastor Livingston," Nathan said. "What can I do for you today?"

"Well, I have almost as many problems as Job, but I only want help on one of those right now. Are you free anytime today?"

Alan meets with Nathan in his firm's well-appointed conference room. He declines coffee and looks around before telling Nathan about the apparent lapse in his homeowner's insurance policy. Nathan asks a few questions, and Alan is glad to have him on his side. One of his concerns is being addressed. If only he can find help for the problem making all others pale in comparison—the whereabouts of Anna.

After leaving the conference room, Alan prays, "Oh, Lord, please let Anna be okay. Keep her in the palm of your mighty hand and fill her with your love and peace. Let her not give up, dear Lord, and help me not to give up either. You are the creator of the universe. Nothing is too hard for you. I believe you will bring Anna home in your time."

Notwithstanding his faith, Alan has not felt so helpless since his days of getting off alcohol. He had thought detox would kill him; instead, Jesus cleaned him up and made a preacher out of him. If only he could have just one drink now, but he cannot after what the Lord has done for him. He might feel helpless, but deep down he knows his God can do more than he can ever think or imagine. How could he even think a drink would help?

As he is driving back to the compound, Alan calls Honcho to discuss whether to hire private help for finding Anna. They meet at the compound's security office. Alan usually feels a bit intimidated by all the surveillance equipment, but now it gives him comfort.

"Hey, Honcho, I am thankful you had my brother's back on the force, and I must say I am also glad he had yours. Before we make any decisions, we will go to the Lord in prayer for wisdom and guidance."

After the prayer and a few minutes of conversation, Honcho said, "I know a man who solved kidnapping cases for the FBI. His name is Aaron 'Mac' McDonald. He is retired and works as a private consultant. I'll call him if you want."

"If you think he is good, call him. I mean no disrespect to Gary and the other law enforcement officers, but I have got to get Anna back!"

Anna reaches a point where she feels the love of Jesus for Mrs. Bosco. She does not, however, feel that way toward her kidnappers. She asks for forgiveness for failing to pray for the men's souls and begins to pray for them. She also asks for the words to say to Mrs. Bosco to lead her to Jesus.

Mrs. Bosco bought her pens and paper. Writing down her thoughts and feelings in letters to her father, husband, and son helps relieve Anna's mental tension.

Sometimes she thinks her world has crashed and only she and Mrs. Bosco survive. Other times, she thinks God stitched her together, but life loosened the stitches so much the stuffing is falling out.

These thoughts remind her to have faith and believe in God. She finds her faith gives her hope and makes her feel like her stitches are tight; her world has not crashed. She knows she cannot make it without hope, without God.

A KIDNAPPING REVIVAL

Alan preaches for the second time since Anna's kidnapping. The previous Sunday service was bizarre, and the dire persecution predictions created fear and panic.

Only seventy-three out of the one hundred and fifty adults who normally attend are present, and eighteen children out of thirty. Alan thought he was prepared for the reduced attendance, but the reality of the fear and panic and the missing people upset him anew. Preaching is already difficult with Anna gone.

"Good morning. Let us go to the Lord in prayer. Father God, we come to you now in the name of your Son Jesus. We worship you. We honor you. We thank you for this day and for your many blessings. We pray for our country, our state, and our community. We pray for the peace of Jerusalem and the body of Christ throughout the world. Lord, we ask for you to guide us and protect us, and we pray for all who are facing persecution for their Christianity. We thank you that you will never leave nor forsake us, and we ask you to help us to stand strong for you. In the mighty name of Jesus. Amen.

"I am saddened but not surprised to see so many empty seats this morning. I want to thank each of you who came. We must pray for our absent members, for God to comfort their hearts and help them overcome their fears by faith. Reach out to them as God leads you and do not condemn them. God will see us through this, and we need to stay strong in him. We want our words and actions to glorify him. We must stay in the center of his will. As Jesus taught us to pray, 'Thy kingdom come, thy will be done.'"

As Alan finishes his sermon, he asks everyone to stay for an informal meeting, at which they decide to continue the Wednesday-night Bible studies. Alan leaves to have lunch with his family, minus Anna, his heart.

Larry and his father continue making progress toward developing a relationship, and Larry hopes to see his father accept Christ as his Lord and Savior. He arrives at the Sunset in a good mood. As he walks over to his dad's bed, he gives him a brief hug and says, "Howdy. You look comfortable. Is Miss Molly still bossing you around?"

"She's pretty nice. I think she enjoyed meeting you. Did you ever marry, son?"

"No."

"I guess after growing up with the constant fighting between your mom and me, and my horrible treatment of you and your sister, you figured marriage was not worth the pain."

Larry turned away from his dad, feeling that familiar stab to his heart. But recovering, he said, "Yes, but I don't hold it against you any longer. Everybody gets a second chance with Jesus. His death would not mean much if we did not. It is only because Jesus gave me a second chance that I can forgive you. You must understand nobody could make me want to forgive you, nobody but Jesus."

"I believe you, son. I can see how you have changed from that angry, foul-mouthed juvenile delinquent you once were. Remember the time you stole that little sports car to impress your girlfriend and ran out of gas about ten miles from town? After walking the ten miles back to town, she left you, and you went to the owner and confessed. He let you work instead of turning you in to the police."

"I've never forgotten Mr. Goldman. He made quite an impression on me, but I was too stupid and hardheaded to stay out of trouble. God's impression on me though will last an eternity. He forgives me even when I mess up and loves me just as much as he always has. He never ceases to amaze me. I could keep talking about Jesus all night, but I have got to go home. My job starts early tomorrow. I'll try to come next weekend."

"You know, son, it means the world to me that you came

back after all I did to you, and your leaving the past behind. Thank you."

Larry leaves, praying to God to spare his father until he accepts Jesus, and he knows his prayer lines up with God's will that no one die without Jesus. He pulls up to the building where he works and lives. He does not make much money, but he thanks God for the job and the place to live.

As he walks down the stairs to get to his quarters, Larry realizes he has not prayed for Jim and Roger. He adds them to his prayers for his father, Alan and his family, and Manny, Esther, and Honcho, plus his new bosses and coworkers and Miss Molly. He is thankful to the Lord and privileged to have so many people to pray for.

Back at the compound, Gary and Beth are thankful for their time alone together.

"Oh, babe," Gary said, "it feels so awesome to be holding you. I might just float right up to heaven if you kiss me."

"Well," Beth said, "I don't want you leaving me, so no kisses for you!"

Gary smiled and gently lifted her chin. "Are you sure?" he murmured as he kissed her slowly and deeply.

"Ah," said Beth, "even if you do float away, I guess it will be worth it. Do that again."

CHAPTER 6

The next morning when Alan arrives at the church, he sees a note taped to his door. Alan enters his office and reads the contents: "If you want to see your wife, you must sign a divorce petition to end your marriage and sign a letter of resignation from your post as pastor of the Good News Methodist Church. If you do not, worse things will happen to you."

Alan pushes his chair back from the desk. He cannot stand it. When Gary shows up, Alan jumps up and says, "Gary, this blows me away! How can I do these things, and what would it mean to someone for me to do them? Why would anyone want me to divorce my wife and resign as pastor?"

"Alan, someone may love your wife and want to marry her legally."

"But who loves my Anna?"

"It might not be someone in love with Anna. Maybe it is an attempt to destroy you by taking away your wife, your home, and your church."

"Gary, what worse things can you think of besides taking my wife and my church and burning my home? Oh, no. What about Riley?"

"I don't know, Alan, but I'll call Honcho and make sure

he keeps a constant eye on the boy and puts the surveillance equipment on high alert."

"What other things can they do to me? And why? What horrible thing did I do? I am a sinner saved by grace. What did I do to get hit with all this?"

Gary said, "It's probably not anything you have done, Alan, but I don't know what it is. I'm going to the station. There may be a fingerprint this time. After I go to the station, I'll head to the compound to see if Honcho needs any help with security."

Alan arrives at Nathan's office in record time. His office has rich, dark wood and a thick Persian rug. These amenities do not reassure Alan, however, who said, "Nathan, did you know my wife was kidnapped; my church was subjected to a madman who scared everyone about being persecuted; and my house was burned? That is why I said I was feeling like Job.

"Now I have received a demand letter from the kidnapper. He wants me to divorce my wife and resign as pastor, or something even worse will happen to me."

Slumping into one of Nathan's cushioned guest chairs, Alan asks with resignation, "What do you think about this, and what would you do?"

"Wow, Alan, I have never known anyone who has lost so much in such a short time. I admire you; you are still standing."

"Not really, at least not without God holding me up."

Nathan gets up from his chair behind the desk and rests his hand on Alan's shoulder, saying, "It sounds to me like someone wants your wife and wants to ruin you for having the woman he wants. Or someone wants to ruin you, and taking away your wife, your home, and your church should produce that result."

Nathan sits down, leans back in his chair, with his full attention devoted to Alan, and says, "You can execute the documents and truthfully claim they were executed under duress, but why should you? Divorce will likely not result in your seeing your wife but, if anything, will allow the kidnapper to marry her legally. Even if he did not marry her, he might convince her you wanted to divorce her."

"She would never believe that!" says Alan, as he groans and holds his stomach. He excuses himself from the office. When he returns and says he is okay, Nathan continues, saying, "As to resigning your role as pastor, I'm not sure what that gets you. It might help protect the church, but it might not."

Nathan moves to a chair beside Alan and says, "If I were you, I would be reluctant to give in to the demands of the kidnapper, but you must make your own decision, which I know you will after you have prayed. Maybe the law enforcement guys will lean on the man they have in custody.

"I'll find out who his lawyer is and give him a call. Of course, as you know, you must take this up with the highest court and judge. I am just a lawyer. I'll do whatever you and the Lord decide should be done."

Nathan places his hand on Alan's back and prays for him to have strength and wisdom.

Alan stares at his desk unseeing, and dark emotions stalk his soul. He knows they will take up residence if he does not seek God's presence to protect him. How easy it would be to try to drown the emotions with alcohol.

He flexes his muscles, shakes his head, and stands up from his desk, whispering a quick thank you to God, who has delivered him yet again.

A KIDNAPPING REVIVAL

Three weeks after the first note, another note arrives, which says, "A young woman in your congregation will publicly accuse you of sexual harassment, and an older member of the church will charge you with embezzlement. If you do not want to face these charges, you know what you must do. You have ten days."

Alan puts his head down on his desk and cries out to God as he wonders if he can carry on. After about an hour of prayer, he feels the peace of God. Then and only then can he meet with others. His first meeting is with Nathan.

"Alan," said Nathan, "we are dealing with a devious but educated mind, not the kidnapper in custody or his partner but their employer, whom they have probably never met and don't know. The problem with these trumped-up charges against you is once they are made public, it may not matter they are not true.

"This brings us to the question of whether you will divorce your wife and resign your church to avoid having your character assassinated. Knowing you for a short time is long enough for me to know your answer will be a resounding no. And I advise you to avoid giving in to the kidnapper's demands. He does not promise to release Anna if you execute the divorce and resignation, and there is no assurance this will be the last demand."

Then Alan meets with Gary, who said, "We may have a lead on the partner of the man in custody, a man named Roger Cutlow. If we find him, we may get somewhere. Also, Mac is looking for people who have grievances against you, and he is investigating Jason Stone.

"You know I love you and Anna so very much, and I know you want to do the right thing by her in this situation. I cannot see any benefit to Anna if you do the divorce and resign from the church. The kidnapper will probably issue more threats. The one good thing about all this is Anna's safety."

Alan heads to the creek where he had taken Riley fishing. He sits with his back to a big oak tree and prays aloud. Then he listens as the Lord speaks to his heart.

After a long time under the tree, Alan concludes he can never divorce his wife, no matter the consequences to him, for God put them together; Alan will not let any man break them up. Likewise, he cannot resign as pastor of his church, for God placed him there; only the church can make him go. With these decisions made, Alan feels the peace of God that "surpasses all understanding" and "guards your heart and mind through Christ Jesus."

Alan meets with the deacons of the church and tells them about the threatened accusations and his options. He says that even if they want him to resign, he will not. They will have to fire him, or let him continue as the pastor, or put him on leave. He will not give in to the criminal's demands.

He asks the church to stand with him; he could divorce his wife and resign from the church, but since those actions contradict the teaching of Jesus, he will subject himself to the false accusations.

To Alan's amazement, most of the deacons believe God will sustain the church, even if the accusations are brought against him. They believe Alan should not give in to the demands, but to Alan's dismay, they place him on leave pending resolution of the charges. They say he needs the time anyway because of his wife's kidnapping.

The deacons who object say Alan is asking too much of the church to support him against sexual harassment and embezzlement charges. They believe the reputation of the church will be irreparably damaged by the charges if he is not fired, adding to the harm already wrought by Jason Stone's pronouncements.

Mrs. Bosco smiles as she pours coffee for Anna and passes her the bowl of fruit.

Anna said, "Mrs. Bosco, you've been good to me, and I appreciate you more than you know. That is why I want to tell you about Jesus. He loves you and wants to have a relationship with you. You will never be alone, for he will always be with you. He will never leave you nor forsake you. Even in your darkest night, he will be with you. Do you want to know him?"

"I must say I admire you, Anna. If I had been kidnapped, I do not think I would have the peace you have or as good an attitude as you, and I guess that peace and hope come from your Jesus."

"Yes, Mrs. Bosco, and he gives me love for you. I pray for you and my kidnappers every day. Jesus wants to save you and them, just as he has saved me."

"Larry, this is Molly at the Sunset Home. Your dad didn't want me to call you, but he had a mild stroke last night."

"I'll come later today. Is it life-threatening?"

"No, but he has several issues. Any one of them or a combination could be fatal at any time."

"I pray he will make a salvation decision soon."

"He asked me a couple of Bible questions. I've tried to help, and I pray for you both."

"Thanks, Molly."

After hanging up, Larry decides to take the time to see his dad right away, so he calls his boss and explains the situation. The boss lets him go with a promise to make it up later that night.

"Hi, Dad. How are you?"

"Not too good today, son. I had a little spell yesterday. Anyway, I am glad you are here. I want you to pray with me to receive the Lord Jesus as my Savior."

"Oh, Dad, let's pray."

They hug after praying and cry tears of joy, tinged with sadness for the lost years. Molly enters the room.

"Oh, hi, Molly. Guess what my dad just did! Thanks for praying!"

Molly grips Mr. Reed's hand. With tears in his eyes, he tells her, "I belong to Jesus now, Molly, and I am ready to go anytime the Lord calls me home."

Molly said, "Jesus will make a huge difference in your life. You've got a good son, Mr. Reed, and you two will get to make up for lost time eternally!"

Mr. Reed asked, "Larry, do you think you could find your sister, Louise? I want to make peace with her and ask her for forgiveness. She reached out to me once, but I did not answer. Without the Lord, I had no reason to talk with her. I do now."

"I doubt I can find her, but I'll give it my best shot."

"That's all I can ask."

Alan drinks in the peace he feels as he walks silently through the empty church pews. Then the phone rings. He rushes to his office, suddenly on hyper alert and panicking. It is Nathan. Alan sinks into his chair as Nathan says, "Hi, Alan. I know you're overwhelmed, but I wondered if you ever found out anything on your homeowner's insurance."

"Yes, I meant to call you. We are one month overdue on a policy that has been in force for over eight years."

"The policy requires the company to mail a notice of intention not to renew the policy, and there is a grace period of thirty-one days for the payment. If you did not receive notice, the grace period has not begun, and your payment now will avoid termination. Send your payment or, better still, take your payment to your local agent today. Then you can file the claim right away."

On his way home, Alan awaits a firing squad. Only he does not know which way it is coming from or who is on the squad. Obviously, people lie. What causes them to lie? They might lie if they hate him, or if they want to get revenge, or if they are threatened. And of course, they might lie for money.

Would the charges against him stand up in court? Or, as Nathan said, would it even matter? The peace he experienced under the oak tree and at the church is slipping away.

How he misses Anna. With her at his side with her godly counsel and so much love, he could face any giant, no matter how big. And he feels the loss of his parents in the car accident six years ago. They, too, provided godly counsel. He prays and gives the whole messed-up situation to God. He will be still and know God.

The deacons voted to place Alan on leave, but they did not find anyone to replace him. While they wait for the district office to act, they allow Alan to preach as usual.

Sunday morning arrives just on time. Alan spent most of his time that week at the church, trying to plant himself firmly on the Rock. He wants and needs God's house, God's Word, God's people, God's love, God's guidance, and, most of all, God himself. After worship and prayer, Alan said, "As stated in first Corinthians, chapter sixteen, verse thirteen, 'Watch, stand fast in the faith, be brave, be strong.' And in Ephesians, chapter six, verse eleven, we are told to 'put on the whole armor of God, that you may be able to stand against the wiles of the devil,' and, in verse thirteen, 'having done all, to stand.'

"We are to stand in the face of fear, for our Lord sustains us. He never lets us down. Even at our lowest points, we will still be standing in our spirits, for our God upholds us; yes, he carries us. He never lets us go. So 'humble yourselves under the mighty hand of God, that he may exalt you in due time, casting all your care upon the Lord, for he cares for you.' That is in first Peter, chapter five, verses six and seven.

"In Psalms, chapter thirty-one, verse three, David says to the Lord, 'You are my rock and my fortress.' In chapter sixty-one, verse two, hear me church, 'when my heart is overwhelmed, lead me to the rock that is higher than I.' Are you planted on the rock this morning, church? Are you standing firm? Is the rock that is higher than you where you stay, or do you go there occasionally like on Sunday mornings? Listen to me; God is a twenty-four-seven God. He loves you no matter what, but do you love him? How do you show him that you love him?"

Alan pauses, gesturing to the musicians, and raising his hands, saying, "Let us close our eyes and lift our hands to our God, thanking him that he is the rock of our salvation. If there is anyone here, as we have all been, who does not know this rock, our refuge, come and meet him today. Come. Do not wait. Come."

The last of the music fades away after Alan talks with the young man who has given his life to Christ. There is no greater miracle, thinks Alan, than that of a soul being snatched from the fires of hell by our awesome God. Alan hugs the young man, prays with him, and is overcome with compassion and transported to that heavenly place where all is right with the world because God reigns.

Alan wrestles with the fear that assaults him when he wakes up in his bed alone in the middle of the night. "Oh, God of the universe, look down on your children and bring us back together if it is your will. In the name of Jesus." He goes back to sleep, and when he wakes up, he takes the day off, like he does every Monday.

CHAPTER 7

Unlike his brother, Gary works on Mondays. This Monday, Gary ignores most of the friendly greetings and pounds his desk with his fists. They have failed to find Jim Boren's partner, Roger Cutlow. Roger seems to have dropped off the face of the earth since they arrested Jim Boren. His disappearance makes Gary think a wealthy nutcase directs all the action from behind the scenes, one who could make someone disappear, temporarily or permanently.

The search for Roger needed to be broader and smarter, but Gary does not know where the net should be cast. Time to talk to his counterpart at the Bureau, Agent Milton Steele.

"Agent Steele, Gary Livingston here. Do you know anything new on our kidnapping case? We seem to have hit a brick wall."

"Hi, Gary," said Milton. "Call me Milton. I assume the kidnapping was engineered by a person or persons unknown to Jim Boren and Larry Reed. Finding Roger Cutlow is a priority. If the accusers against Alan's character come forward, they may be able to identify other criminals involved. We'll help you what we can."

"Mac, I'm Gary Livingston. Thank you for coming. How's the investigation going?"

"I have not found anyone yet who fits the role of kidnapper or arsonist or even gives me a reason to look twice, but I still have a way to go. As you know, hate and greed and other strong emotions can last many years, sometimes becoming an obsession or psychosis. So, I am going back to Alan's and Anna's school days—students and teachers and coaches, as well as church friends and so forth. It's a lengthy process, but I don't want to miss anybody."

"I want you to be as thorough as possible for those very reasons and because the police force is shorthanded and could never investigate as you can. How about Jason Stone?"

"I'll have a report on him soon. Should I give Alan that report directly?"

"Yes, Alan can better understand that report, and as far as I know, Stone has not violated any laws.

"Honcho said you are the best, Mac, and I trust Honcho, so I trust you. If you find anything we can use in our investigation, please let me know."

In response to his father's request for Larry to find his sister, Larry researches several nights at the local library. When he had about given up, he finds her. The next afternoon, on break, Larry gives her a call and is surprised he recognizes her voice.

"Louise," Larry said, "it has been a long time, but you sound the same as you always did. Do you remember me?"

"Of course, Larry, I remember you. How did you find me?"

"It wasn't easy. I had to rent a booth at the library," he said, thinking if she knew what he had done for the past ten years, she would hang up.

"Ha-ha!" she said. "What do you look like now?"

"As ugly as ever. Are you married?"

"Yes, Larry, I've been married for eight years to Seth Marks. He is a good man, nothing like our father, and we have two beautiful girls. Susan is seven, and Marilyn is five. How about you?"

Larry says, "Not married, no kids. I called you because I reconnected with Dad. He is sorry he was a bad parent and wants to make peace with you. I forgave him, and he and I are becoming close."

Louise did not respond at first, and Larry thought she might have hung up. Then she said, "Larry, that sounds completely crazy—the two of you having a close relationship. He was so horrible to you, all that pain you suffered, all those nights you cried yourself to sleep. Not to mention what he did to me. He cannot say anything to make me want to see him, much less reconcile with him. And you forgave him? Are you being straight with me?"

Larry says, "Yeah, I asked the Lord into my heart. I am a Christian if you can believe that! And since Dad may not be around much longer, I told him how I changed; it was the Lord's doing. And he became a Christian too."

"You couldn't surprise me more, Larry, than if you'd said you were running for president! I guess if you forgave him, I should not say never, but it would be hard for me to forgive him. I had nightmares for years."

Larry is surprised, too, over the changes in his dad, but he knows all the credit belongs to the God of the impossible. He said, "I had no idea you suffered so much, but it's all true, Louise. I forgave him, and he believes Jesus is real since I told him it was only because of Jesus I could forgive him. I believe you can too. All that hate takes a toll. He is not the monster he was, just as I am no longer the criminal I have been. Can't you come see Dad—and me too, of course? He may not be in this world much longer."

"I don't know, Larry. The girls are busy, and Seth has crazy hours. Maybe I can get away for a day or two. Seth is a lawyer for Raytheon and works more than most corporate lawyers. The girls are involved in all kinds of sports and other activities. And

I work too, you know. I went back to school and made a teacher of myself, but I am not teaching summer school. Can you believe I'm a teacher?"

"Sounds like you are doing great. I am proud of you, Louise. I have not done very well myself. My greatest accomplishment so far is staying alive—well, besides accepting Jesus, but that is all about him. Let me know when you can come. It's so great to reconnect with you, and I can't wait to meet my brother-in-law and nieces."

Alan heads home early to spend time with Riley. Waiting for the latest threatened assault on his life and career zaps what little energy he has.

Riley runs right into his arms when Alan arrives. Alan's energy comes back to him, and a smile brightens his long, mournful face.

"Daddy, how come you are home? Didn't you go to work at the church?"

"I just wanted to see you, Riley. How about we play miniature golf?"

"Yeah, Daddy, go putt-putt!"

Riley holds Alan's hand and does not let go. He follows him to his room and regales him with the day's events. *What a precious boy*, Alan thinks. *Thank you, Lord, for my son. Help me to be the father he needs* he prays with a thankful heart.

"Come on, sport. We will see if Honcho wants to go with us."

"Honcho, do you want to join us in a game of putt-putt golf?"

"Absolutely. I'll beat you both, and you can buy me ice cream for my prize!"

"No, Mr. Honcho, I'll beat you!"

"No," said Alan, "I'm going to beat you both!"

Meanwhile, Gary meets with Mac at the local bakery. They

have coffee and muffins and sit across from each other in a booth. Inhaling the delicious aromas, Mac said, "A few individuals deserve a second look. So, now I am in the process of interviewing people acquainted with these individuals. Alan and Anna are well thought of by most of their associates, going all the way back to grade school. Having made quite a few enemies myself along the way, I am impressed."

"One reason you're the man for the job, Mac, is because none of the associates recognize you, and they don't know you are investigating the kidnapping. What's your cover?"

"I tell them I am a writer. It works. People like talking to writers."

"Well, keep up the good work, and tell me if you need any resources. You may get a call from time to time from Honcho or me. I can pay your fee along the way if you need me to."

"Good. I cannot wait on the fee until the end of the case, but I do not want to put any more pressure on Alan. A lesser man would have thrown in the towel by now."

As Mac leaves the meeting, he thinks about his attempt to write a novel in his retirement. He needs the extra money to help care for his wife, who has Alzheimer's. She still recognizes Mac and their children. Mac experienced the disease with his mother, and he knows the toll the disease exacts on the one with the disease and all the family. Their youngest daughter stays with her mother to allow Mac to work.

Later, when Mac arrives home, his wife is asleep, so he calls Alan.

"Hi, Alan. This is Mac. I told Gary that I would report to you on my investigation of Jason Stone. Is this a good time?"

Riley was sleeping, so Alan said, "Go right ahead, Mac.

I'm listening." Alan rarely spoke on the phone without doing something, so he folded clothes.

Mac said, "Jason's father was a preacher who garnered much criticism from his congregation, other churches, and members of the community because of his anti-Semitic and anti-Catholic remarks. The elder Stone, however, labeled the criticism as Christian persecution, even though Christians did the criticizing. He painted himself the victim, and he would not accept correction. After a bitter fight, the church dismissed him from his position as pastor, and he and his family moved away.

"Your parents led the effort to fire Stone while others wanted him to stay. They succeeded in getting him fired.

"His wife and son took Reverend Stone's dismissal hard. They bore the cruel consequences of his actions. She was ostracized from the community, and Jason was taunted at school. Eventually, Stone found work in a factory in another town, and the only thing left of his days as a preacher was a painful memory."

Alan paused in folding, reacting to Reverend Stone's blasphemy, shaking his head, saying, "I can understand Jason better after hearing about his childhood, though his actions at the church still defy logic."

"Well, by the time Jason left home, he believed God had ordained him to warn churches about Christian persecution. Whether Jason believes as his dad did about Jews and Catholics is not known, as he does not place blame on any one group. He says persecution of Christians is coming, which is true. He may deliver his message in a way that is unorthodox, but it is not criminal."

Alan asks, "Do you think Jason's message at Good News is related to the kidnapping and the arson? The timing is certainly suspect."

"Alan, it seems unlikely that Jason Stone has any connection to the kidnapping of Anna or the other attacks against you. The warning to the church came at a bad time, but other than the timing, there is nothing to connect it. I do not know if Jason made this speech in other churches or if Good News is the only one. Some say he did, and others say he did not. I haven't called the churches yet."

"Thank you for your report, Mac. Your ability to find information and your attention to detail impress me. We may find a connection to the kidnapping later."

Fewer people attend the Wednesday-night service than Alan hopes. He figures time will lessen the Jason Stone effect, but it has not happened yet. He thanks God that no known incidents of persecution had happened locally, and he still believes God will bring revival.

"What is faith? Faith is when the world comes crashing down on you, but you do not despair, for you have faith in God. Faith is when your family is falling apart, but you believe that all will be well, for you have faith in God. Faith is what rises in your spirit when there is a problem at work or school or home and you say, 'God's got this.'

"'Now faith is the substance of things hoped for, the evidence of things not seen.' That is verse one of chapter eleven of Hebrews. According to Matthew, chapter seventeen, verse twenty, we can move mountains if we have faith and do not doubt. So, how much faith do we need? That same verse says our faith can be the size of a mustard seed and still move mountains."

Alan finishes his talk on faith, prays, and the head of the deacons come up to him and gesture for privacy. He then said, "Alan, we have been advised Brother Charles Winters will replace you during your time on leave, starting Sunday."

Alan's mouth flies open, and he stops in his tracks because he is shocked Charles will stand behind his pulpit.

Feeling doubt assailing his faith, Alan says to the head deacon, "What about my salary?"

"You will be paid for the first three months, and then we will go from there."

Alan nods, but he feels rejection rather than appreciation. What he would give for a drink, he thinks, and then repents.

That afternoon, Larry picks Louise up at the Memphis airport. "Hi, sis. You made it. You look great!"

"You look older than I expected, Larry. Living hard?"

"Flattery will get you nowhere, Louise."

"Ha, let's get me somewhere and eat—my treat—and then visit Dad once we have a chance to talk."

"Can't take you to my place, but there's a motel near the home where Dad is staying."

After a meal at a country restaurant, Larry and Louise visit their dad. Louise stands defiantly at the foot of his bed, giving him an occasional glance. She wants to be ready to walk out quickly. They talk for a while. She tells him about her family and her accomplishments, as if to say she had made it notwithstanding his abuse. He tells her about the accident that left him disabled and unable to live alone.

When they exhaust these subjects, Louise turns, preparing to go, and her father says through tears, "I do not deserve it, Louise, but I ask you to forgive me. I regret the things I said and did, and I will understand if you can't forgive me."

It takes her a few moments to recover from the shock she experiences at his apology. It is not what she expected. She stands still, realizing she feels compassion for him and forgives him. The freedom she feels takes her by surprise too, and she smiles at her dad, for the first time she can remember. Larry leaves the two of them together and goes to work with a happy heart.

A KIDNAPPING REVIVAL

Alan is coming apart. He realizes his life will again be turned upside down when they make the threatened accusations. His only defense is his innocence. *Who will make the accusations and how? Will they hold press conferences? Will they go to the police? Will the police arrest me? What will my church members think? The community? Oh, God, please help me!*

CHAPTER 8

Anna throws down her pen and scatters the letters she is writing to her family. She jumps up, kicks the mattress, and jerks the cover off the bed. Not only is she away from her husband and her child and the rest of her family and friends, but she also misses her patients and her coworkers. The deadline for getting into the master's program in nursing passed right after her kidnapping.

Her life is changed from one of love and a comfortable routine to one of total uncertainty. Physically, she cannot complain, except the missing windows make her feel cut off from everything, which she is. Psychologically, she is a wreck. Without Riley to hug her neck and give her a sloppy kiss, and Alan to give her a slow and gentle kiss, she feels abandoned. She misses them terribly. But she has the love of the Lord. No one can take that away from her. Without God, she would have already given in to despair.

She wonders if any demands for ransom had been made—and the response. She believes Alan would give anything—everything—for her freedom. But it seems long enough for things to have worked out.

She wants to cry out to God, scream at him, for letting this happen. She believes "all things worked together for good," but she cannot see how any of this could work together for good. It all seems bad. He will work things out; she believes; she will try not to doubt.

"Louise, I wish you could stay with us longer," said Larry. "Dad will miss you. Do you think you can bring the family next time? It would mean so much to him—and to me!"

"I'll find out when I can come back and if I can bring the family. I had a great time visiting with you and Dad. I can't thank you enough for getting in touch with me."

"Thank Dad for getting us back together. It was the one request he made of me after his stroke. His eyes sparkled when you forgave him, Louise, and I am glad we are all Christians.

"Safe travels! Tell your children their uncle Larry wants to meet them. Also tell Seth I'm looking forward to meeting him and discussing all those Old Testament passages I don't understand."

Gary decides to question Jim Boren about Roger Cutlow, and surprisingly, Jim wants to talk, perhaps because of the days behind bars. Gary makes sure he gets all the required waivers.

From the interview, Gary learns Roger was raised by his mother; his father was unknown. He left home at sixteen and never returned. He had no siblings, and his mother had also been an only child.

Jim said, "I never saw Roger with family or friends. I am not sure he had any. We worked together on two or three burglaries. This was our first kidnapping. Roger got directions from someone else, but he never told me who was calling the shots. I am not sure he knew. I have no idea where you might find Roger. Hiding is one of his best skills."

Gary knows little useful information came from the interview, but it did confirm the existence of someone in charge who pays the guys to do the work, and it established Jim and Roger as the perpetrators of the kidnapping.

Larry gets another call from Molly. He wonders what she will say this time, afraid of what might have happened to his father. But what she says blesses his socks right off his feet. He does his best breakdancing routine, for she invites him to a social at the home.

Larry is still dancing, at least in his spirit. Molly sways to imaginary music and gives Mr. Reed a kiss on his forehead. Mr. Reed is dressed in his best clothes, including a bow tie. Larry realizes how much his life has improved since he gave it to the Lord. He thanks the Lord and then asks again for forgiveness for his former life. He wants to tell other people about Jesus. He remembers the night when Alan challenged him to evaluate his life and how that made all the difference.

Alan answers the door and says, "Come in. I am glad you came by, Larry. You are one of the bright spots in a very dark period of my life."

"Well, the brightness came from your introduction of Jesus into my life, Pastor Alan, and God has turned my life around. I have an honest job and a place to live. My father and sister and I have reconnected after years of separation and hostility. A sweet girl asked me to a social at the home where my father lives. What more can I say! God is so good to me, and I am an undeserving sinner saved by grace! Thank you, Pastor Alan."

"No, thank you, Larry, for listening to the Lord and following up on his offer of eternal life. Not to discourage you, but tribulation will occur. Take a stand for the Lord even when hard times come. It's ironic, but sometimes people forget the Lord when they succeed, and I am glad to see you are praising him."

"Pastor Alan, I pray for you and Riley and your wife. I cannot imagine how awful the situation is, notwithstanding your strong faith. Is there anything I can do to help you?"

"Thank you, Larry. God has blessed you, and I thank you for your prayers. I cannot think of anything you can do, but your prayers mean a lot to me."

"Stay another minute or two. Riley will want to see you before you go."

"Hey, Riley, are you keeping everybody straight?"

"Yes, sir. I miss seeing you."

"I miss you too, Riley. I have a job, so I stay busy and spend some time with my daddy like you do. I'll see you later."

Esther clears the kitchen table, and Beth gives Riley his bath. Then Alan gets Riley into bed for story time. Riley has learned to read some of the words, much to his and his daddy's delight.

Once Riley falls asleep, Alan tries to think about good things God brought forth from this horrible situation: Larry's salvation; Beth's and Gary's relationship with their nephew; his connection with his congregation; and the time he gets to spend with his brother and his son. He also appreciates Honcho more. And though painful, he has reevaluated his life and his roles as husband, father, brother, friend, and pastor, and he finds himself lacking in all the roles. He is determined to improve, especially as a husband, when he gets the opportunity.

Larry hangs around with Honcho. Honcho cared for Larry when he stayed at the compound and helped him find his father. As Larry gets ready to leave, someone throws a stone at Riley's bedroom window. A person takes off running, and Honcho lets the dogs out. Larry jumps back when Honcho lets the dogs out. He does not trust dogs, and his heart pounds when they dart past.

The dogs did their job, and the intruder is subdued when

Honcho gets to him and said, sternly, "Okay, son, what's your name?"

"Randy Byrne."

"What are you doing here? Why did you throw a stone at the house?"

"I was paid a hundred dollars."

"Who paid you?"

"A man stopped me when I was riding my bike."

"What did he look like?"

"I don't know. He wore a dark hoodie with the hood pulled over his head."

"What did he say exactly?"

"He said he needed me to scare somebody. He told me which window to throw the rock at. He said he would come back and get me if I did not throw the rock. I never made that much money, and I believed him. He looked mean—you know, his eyes."

"I thought you couldn't see his face. What color were his eyes?"

"Kind of black."

"How did you slip in without being seen?"

"He told me to wait for a car to turn in and hide myself with the car, so when I saw this car turning in, I crouched down and ran along its side. I was told to wait until the car was leaving, so I would not be seen and so it would look like someone in the car threw the rock. I guess I did not do that part too good; I got in a hurry. You got some smart dogs. Am I in trouble?"

"You'll have to go down to the police station. They will question you."

"The police!" he almost shouted. "My dad will kill me!"

"Well, you should have thought about that when you took the money and agreed to sneak in and throw the stone."

"I guess whatever happens to me is because I'm an idiot."

"Just tell the truth, and you may get cut some slack. They will keep you locked up until your father comes. He may decide to let you spend the rest of the night there."

Alan yells at Honcho as soon as he hears what happened, saying, "I thought our security is the best, and yet a thirteen-year-old kid manages to beat it! How can that happen, Honcho? If something bad happens to Riley, I'll die."

Honcho responds immediately to the threat, but Alan wants more advance security. Honcho agrees to add cameras, another member to the staff to monitor the video feed, and another security guard at the gate.

Then he creates a new system. The security guards will stop and search all vehicles outside the gate, and the occupants will be brought into the compound by the guards in vans. No vehicles will be allowed on the property other than the vehicles of the residents. Additional cameras to capture the space around the vehicles are also added.

Honcho thinks the kidnapper just meant to torture Alan with the rock-throwing stunt. They all agree, however, that even the slightest indication of danger to Riley is reason to arm the place like Fort Knox.

Alan withdraws from Honcho and the others in a subdued and thoughtful mood. He goes to his room and closes his door. There are only four days until his sanity will be attacked again. He is not ready, nor can he ever be ready. If not for his faith in God, he would never make it through.

CHAPTER 9

Hank Richards takes the two accusers, Mary Jo Holt and Joel Benton, from their homes to an abandoned building in a deserted area of Tupelo. He starts with Mary Jo, while his partner, Jeff Hanson, holds Mr. Benton in the vehicle.

Hank looks around at all the tools and plays with a hammer while he says, "Mary Jo, you will hold a press conference in four days. You will dress conservatively and be prepared to cry. Explain how Brother Livingston's status as a pastor affected you when he tried to grope and kiss you in his office, giving the impression you thought it was maybe wrong to turn him down."

Mary Jo struggles to breathe and does not look at him. She is afraid. He leers at her as he continues, saying, "Make sure they know his attack on you damaged you, ruined your trust in preachers, and undermined your faith in God. It made you question him and his sincerity in his counseling. Maybe you should not have trusted him when he gave you and your husband advice. How could he do this to you? You are suffering from depression because of his sexual assault."

Mary Jo jumps when Hank throws the hammer against a metal cabinet. Laughing, he said, "Do you think you can handle this, Mary Jo? We cannot have any mistakes. If you have any questions, ask them now. We will not tolerate failure. Your sister's life is at stake. Think of that during the press conference, and you should be able to cry."

"Where will the press conference be?" Mary Jo asked.

"At a lawyer's office. Here is the address and phone number. Be there an hour before the press conference to go over your statement. The lawyer will also go with you to the police station, where you will file a complaint."

Jeff brings Mr. Benton in and takes Mary Jo out. Hank sees that Mr. Benton hides his nervousness better than Mary Jo. He said, "Mr. Benton, be ready to go to the police within a week. We will let you know exactly when the day before. On the day you file the complaint, you will be represented by an attorney who will meet with you that morning. I'll give you more information about him when I call you with the date and time."

"I don't understand how I can accuse Pastor Alan of embezzlement," said Mr. Benton. "He is an honest man."

"Our accountants are quite certain he has been siphoning money from the building fund for the past two years at least, maybe longer. It is your duty to turn him in. A pastor should be above reproach. Yours is not. He is a thief."

"I would like to see the accounting report. If it proves me wrong and he is guilty, I want him prosecuted to the full extent of the law."

"Certainly. I will have it delivered to you later today. Remember the motivation to do a good job of making this charge stick. You don't want anything bad to happen to that sweet grandchild."

Hank and his partner, Jeff Hanson, return Mary Jo and Mr. Benton to their homes with final warnings. After they let them out of the van, Jeff said, "Do we trust these people, Hank? They can identify us!"

"Don't worry, man, we've got that covered," said Hank as he let a cigarette. "Mary Jo and Benton each have family they want to protect. If they give us any trouble, the 'accidents' will be tragic.

They will not endanger their family members. And both have their own reasons for being quiet.

"Mary Jo is fighting mad at the pastor for telling her she should forgive her husband for cheating on her. Her accusation is a fabrication, but she wants revenge. Benton will believe he is telling the truth after he sees the report. Once he is convinced the pastor is guilty, he will want the pastor to get what is coming to him. In any event, if things go south, we can leave town with enough money to lie low for a long time."

"I wish I felt as confident as you. How do we know we will get paid? When do we get the money?"

"We will be paid half of our fee after the press conference on the sexual assault and half after the embezzlement charge. The funds will be placed into our accounts. Remember, the kidnapper has ordered no deaths, and I do not think he will. We'll be okay."

"I sure hope you're right, Hank. I do not want to give up my life for money. I don't have any big plans, but I'd like to live long enough to get a few things right."

"Are you getting soft on me, Jeff?"

"No. I get tired of it all sometimes. Don't pay me any attention."

"Anna," said Mrs. Bosco, "do you need something new to read or a new movie to watch? I know you must be bored since you worked so many hours before you ended up here."

"Yes, I would love some new reading material. I'll look something up if you'll let me use a computer."

"Sorry, dear, I can't do that. I will print a list of books for you."

"Mrs. Bosco, do you know if any ransom has been demanded for my release?"

"You know as much as I do about what's going on. Try not to think about what might or might not happen."

"You are right, Mrs. Bosco, because God is in control. I gave my life to him some time ago, and my desire is to do his will and for his will to be done in my life. I will not despair, for I trust God to protect me and my family. God is faithful even when I am not. He loves me even when I am not lovely or loving.

"He loves you too, Mrs. Bosco. No one will ever love you as much as the Lord loves you. You are so special to him. He wants a relationship with you, his child. And all it takes to have that relationship is for you to ask Jesus to forgive you of your sins, to save you, and for his spirit to live in your heart. Do you want to do that today, Mrs. Bosco?"

"Not today."

Mac goes to the church to give Alan an update on Jason Stone. He finds Alan at the copying machine trying to fix a paper jam.

"Maybe this isn't a good time to talk," said Mac.

"No, it's a perfect time. Your talking will help me hold onto my sanity, what little I have left."

"Okay, I heard Jason Stone received a large sum of money, source unknown. He spent some on clothes and household appliances, and he traded vehicles. His neighbors noticed his spending, for he is normally very frugal.

"Charles Winters told me Stone visited Good News first and then visited other churches. According to Charles, Stone reached out to the pastors and spoke quietly, with respect, at their services. The congregants were not scared and were appreciative of his message. Charles also said he thought Stone had inherited the money from his family."

Alan moves them into his office, having solved the paper problem.

Mac said, "I believe Stone is sincere about Christian persecution. He might also be susceptible to manipulation and money. I am not sure I believe what Charles is saying—that he received the money from his family. But if not, is someone financing Stone's activities? Is the kidnapper?

"I left a message for Gary about Stone and whether the police will bring a charge against him. I haven't heard back."

"It sounds like you are coming around to the view that Jason may be on the kidnapper's payroll," said Alan.

"Yes, it makes more sense as his source of income. Plus, I do not believe Jason appeared at any church besides yours, as Charles claims. I checked with area churches, and none of them has even heard of Jason Stone."

The men stand and shake hands. Alan said, "Thank you, Mac. Your support means more than I can say. I am interested in why Stone made his bizarre appearance at the church, but my main interest is finding my wife. "I'd be lying if I said the threatened accusations don't concern me too. They bother me a great deal, though I know God will see me through. I may want you to switch your focus to the accusers. I'll let you know."

Alan calls Gary but gets his voicemail, so he leaves a message. He does not know what to do next. He drives to the church for some Bible study and prayer time, but his mind keeps straying to the upcoming accusations.

Once he arrives at the church, his spirits lift. Being in God's house affected him this way when he surrendered to the Lord, and it still does. As he goes toward his office, he sees Corinne filing papers in the cabinet by the window. He realizes he should bring her up to date.

When he begins the discussion, she closes the cabinet door and says, "Brother Alan, I know you didn't steal any money or sexually assault anyone. I pray for discernment, and God has gifted me, so I can read people. I have prayed, and I have total peace about you. I have no doubts and will help in whatever way I can."

"Corinne, you cannot imagine how much I need affirmation today. Thank you. Your confidence in me gives me peace."

Alan spends time in the church library and leaves at the end of the day, his spirit buoyed by the presence of the Lord and the words of his secretary. God is so good to him, and he does not deserve it.

The next morning, Alan said, "Riley, how about I stay home today and spend some time with you."

Riley responds by hugging his dad and saying, "Yay, Daddy. Can we go fishing?"

"You read my mind. The fish probably cannot wait for us to get there! We will have breakfast, dig some worms, grab our poles, and head to the creek.

"Honcho, do you want to go fishing with Riley and me this morning?"

"Yes, fishing with you sounds great. I can be ready in about an hour. I will check in with the new gal monitoring the video feed and the new security guard. Then I will meet you out back. If you want to go on and let me join you after a while, that might work better. You wouldn't have to wait, and I wouldn't have to hurry."

"Okay, we will head to the creek. You come whenever you can join us."

"Aunt Beth made waffles, and she's got blueberries and whipping cream."

"We will eat. Then we will dig some worms."

Larry and Molly visit Mr. Reed. They stand close together, holding hands.

"You two seem to have taken a liking to one another. Glad you came to see the old man."

"We always have time for you, Pops! And you see Molly more than I do. I'm looking for a new job where I can make more money and find a better place to live."

"Maybe you should apply here," said Molly. "I hear they need a handyman and janitor combined. They pay more, and they also provide health insurance."

"Maybe I'll do that. What do you think, Dad? Think you would get tired of me every day? Maybe I should ask Molly that question."

"Now, Larry," Molly said, "I wouldn't have suggested the job to you if I didn't want to see you every day."

"Dad, we're going out for a bite to eat, and Molly will come back to work. Do you want us to bring you lunch?"

"No, son, but thanks for asking."

While driving to the restaurant, Larry said, "Molly, I need to get something off my chest. I am getting serious about you, and I need you to know I have not been a choir boy. In fact—"

Molly interrupts, saying, "Larry, I have a pretty good idea of what you are going to say, but before you do, let me tell you some things that may make you want to stop seeing me. I have not always been as good as you may think. In fact, I spent time in juvenile detention for shoplifting. My family was poor, but that didn't give me an excuse to steal."

Molly squirms in her seat, checks her nails, and looks out the window before saying, "I also was—and this is much harder to admit—a call girl for about two years after I graduated from high school. If I had not heard a street preacher in Memphis, I might still be hustling. But I gave my life to Christ that same night. I ran away from the people who sponsored me and made my way home. Jesus washed my sins away and made me white as snow."

Larry reaches for her hands and says, "Oh, Molly, thank you for sharing. My past life of hating my father, stealing, not because

I needed anything but just for the thrill of it, is much worse, not to mention working for the kidnapper. And Jesus has done the same for me."

They enter the restaurant, both feeling vulnerable and exposed. The food looks less tempting than usual, and Larry almost suggests leaving. Instead, he hands Molly a tray and takes his own.

When they reach their seats and pray over the food, Molly pushes her tray aside and says, "Larry, I'll understand if you want to stop seeing me. Believe me, I feel so much shame. I can see where others would think bad of me and be unable to trust me in a romantic relationship. It will hurt if you decide you can't go on, but I'll understand."

Larry took a sip of his sweet iced tea and said, "Molly, telling me took a lot of courage. I am not going to judge you, and I hope you will not judge me. As God has forgiven us, who are we not to forgive? I hope the fact you told me means you care for me maybe as much as I care for you."

"Thank you, Larry, so much for being so, uh, sweet to me. No one has ever been as understanding as you have. I am getting serious about you, too, and I am glad we are together. And now I'm hungry!"

"Wow, Dad, that's a big fish!"

"Yes, and I think that about does it for me. How about you, Honcho?"

"Yes, Alan, I'm ready to go whenever you two are."

"Riley, we're going back to the house and give these fish to Aunt Beth. She might cook them for our supper tonight. She probably already has something fixed for lunch."

As Riley ran ahead excitedly, Alan held up three fingers and said, "Honcho, there's only three more days before my accusers come out against me, and I don't know what will happen. I will need you and Gary and Beth to continue to look after Riley, as I know you will. I'm just going through all this in my mind, and it's hard to wrap my head around being in jail!"

Honcho said, "You know Riley is our priority. That will never change, whether you are around or not. I don't imagine you'll be put in jail though."

Alan kneels to pray at the altar. When he finishes, he realizes he is not alone. Joel Benton is sitting in a pew with his head down.

"Good afternoon, Mr. Benton."

"Oh, hi, Pastor. How are you?"

"God is still on the throne. If you want to talk, come join me in the library."

Alan has the distinct feeling Mr. Benton wants to talk, but he does not come to the library.

Leaving the church and stopping by the police department, Alan finds Gary in his office. He said, "Things are about to come down around my head. Are you ready to see your brother do the perp walk?"

"Alan, I hope you won't get arrested, but even if you do, don't worry, little brother; I've got your back."

"I'm not asking for favors, even though I want to. I'm glad you'll be here."

Alan heads to the compound. He has been reading about end-times and tribulation while he was at the church. Now, his mind enters a time warp—the end of time, and he is separated from his wife. Why doesn't he just end his life? Or maybe just numb himself to the pain? This is not new for him. Before he knew Jesus, he bought a gun, got drunk, and wrote a letter to his parents, but God intervened in the form of his best friend, who showed up just in time.

How can he consider ending his life now? He loves Jesus, and he loves Anna. Oh, how he misses her. As the song says, she truly is the sunshine of his life.

Who is the weirdo who wants him to divorce Anna? How can the kidnapper find people to accuse Alan of crimes he did not commit? Surely this part of the plan will enable law enforcement to uncover the identity of this criminal. Alan calls Nathan.

"Hi, Nathan. Only three days left until my freedom will be in question. Are you going to be available to bail me out or represent me or do whatever the legal situation requires?"

"Hi, Alan. You caught me before I headed out the door. I will indeed be available, and if there are issues, we will be ready. All you need to do is call me, and I will be there. Most likely, you will not be charged right away, and not at all, unless there is enough evidence to justify an arrest, and there won't be."

"Thank you. I am glad you are my attorney, especially since we have the same Boss. I'll talk with you later."

As he heads back to the compound for some of Beth's fish and hushpuppies, Alan feels so much love for his extended family that he pulls over to a farmer's market and buys gifts for everyone.

"Hi, Dad. How are you?"

"I'm not doing too well, son, what with my wife of forty-five years gone, and my only girl gone, and my mind almost gone. I've just about given up on life altogether."

"Don't give up. Anna needs you. She will be back. Think how devastated she would be if you were not here. And Riley needs you. Beth has brought him here a few times lately, hasn't she?"

"Yes, and I've enjoyed the little fellow. He reminds me of Anna when she was that age, full of wonder and full of energy. He likes to play with the cats and always wants me to play checkers. Before long, I imagine we will switch to chess. He's a sharp boy."

"The kidnapping took an unexpected turn," said Alan, and he proceeded to explain the situation.

"My goodness, Alan, what strange demands. The accusations are ludicrous. What will you do?"

"I don't know. I talked to my lawyer, Nathan Horowitz, and have him on call. Gary will make sure proper procedures are followed. Other than prayer, I do not know what else to do. Do you have any ideas?"

"No, Alan, but I'm praying too. I pray for Anna and you and Riley already, but I will add this prayer and make it a priority."

"Thank you. Why don't you come home with me? Beth is frying fish and making hushpuppies, and she always makes too much, and Riley would be thrilled to see you. How about it?"

"My automatic response is 'no,' but I'll surprise myself this time and say 'yes.' I'd love to come, but you'll have to bring me home."

"No problem. Come on."

The next morning, Alan gets up from a restless night, the kind of night preachers are not supposed to have. If fear is the root of nighttime restlessness, and "perfect love casts out fear," he either does not have perfect love--the love of Jesus--or enough faith. *But he is high on God, so why the restless night?*

"Good morning, everyone. What are we having for breakfast, Beth? Just two more days of freedom, and I intend to enjoy them!"

"What's freedom, Daddy?"

"It means being able to do what you want or need to do without anybody holding you back."

"Like when I want to eat candy before supper?"

"Yes, just like that. You want to do it, but we tell you no. You don't have the freedom to eat candy before supper."

"Come on, you two," said Beth. "Let's say the blessing and eat."

"God is great. God is good. Let us thank him for this food. Amen."

"Very good, Riley. We have plenty of food, so, everybody, dig right in."

Alan starts tying up the loose ends of his life in case the worst happens. He calls his insurance carrier, and his agent comes on the line.

"Hi, Alan. I was just getting ready to call you. The company decided to accept your payment as continuing the coverage under the policy. Now all we are waiting on is the investigator. The fire has been determined to be arson, and you must be eliminated as a suspect before the claim can be paid."

Alan hardly reacts to the suggestion that he may have burned his own home. *What is another accusation?* he thinks as he realizes how close he came to yelling at the agent.

He pays his bills two months in advance. Fortunately, the hospital is paying Anna's salary pursuant to their K&R policy while she is a kidnapping victim. He does not know how long the policy will pay. The church plans to pay him for three months. He would have to adjust when these sources ended. *Enough worry for now*, he thought as he went to the church to spend some time in God's Word, even though Charles would probably be there.

"Why, hello, Corinne. I didn't expect to see you today."

"Hi, Pastor. I just came in to help get Brother Charles get ready for Vacation Bible School."

"When is it?"

"Next week, Sunday through Wednesday nights. The theme is Running with Jesus. I'm helping with the sets and posters and such."

"Sounds great! Thank you for all you do for the Lord and this church," he says as he starts collecting his things from the office. Before he leaves, Charles arrives.

"Charles, how are you today?"

"Probably better than you."

"I actually have some good news. The home insurer decided we had coverage at the time of the house fire. The only problem is the investigators found the fire was deliberately set, so the claim will not be paid until I am off the list of suspects."

When Alan gets back to the compound, Riley is already asleep. He speaks to Honcho, saying, "I may not come home at all on Friday, depending on what my accusers and the police do to me."

Honcho said, "Don't worry about Riley's safety. He is my priority. I watch him twenty-four-seven. Everything will be well taken care of, Alan." Alan thanks him and then speaks with Gary, receiving further consolation and assurance all would be taken care of in his absence, and the priority is still to find Anna.

Anna's life is still frustrating, but as time passes, she fights with less intensity. Not that she accepts her situation, she just manages not to stay demoralized and depressed. Spending hours each day in prayer gives her peace and makes her feel her Lord's presence more than ever.

She hopes Alan experiences a greater closeness to God from this trial in their lives. And sweet Riley, what good is he experiencing? No matter what happens, she believes God's promise to make good out of bad.

Mrs. Bosco had been quieter than usual the past few days. Anna said, "Mrs. Bosco, have I said anything to offend you?"

"No, Anna. I just do not feel like talking. Nothing is wrong."

"Well, I am here for you if you want."

Anna questions whether the wide gap between them will ever be bridged. She prays for God to intervene and to change Mrs. Bosco's heart.

CHAPTER 10

When Friday morning arrives, Alan has a tenuous hold on his peace. Publication of the accusations is due. It is clear to Alan, however, that no accusation, no matter how bad, would ever be as damaging to him as Anna missing.

"Alan," said Gary, "there is breaking news on channel nine."

Alan joins Gary in front of the television in the kitchen. The breaking news is Mary Jo accusing him of sexually assaulting her. The reporter said, "The pastor is Alan Livingston, of the Good News Methodist Church. Livingston's wife was kidnapped three weeks ago from their home, which has since been destroyed by fire. Ms. Holt said the assault occurred when she went to see the pastor about her marriage."

Alan said, "Do you think she will file a complaint with the police?"

"Well, it will be up to her. The guys down at the station will call me if she shows up."

"This sexual assault complaint bothers me on several levels. First, how could she have made up such a thing? I still cannot believe this is happening. Second, it will be her word against mine. Doesn't a criminal charge have to be proved beyond a reasonable doubt?"

"Yes. It's very unlikely any prosecutor would ever take this case to trial," Gary said.

"I pray God will change her heart or show supernaturally she is lying. I cannot prove I'm innocent."

"You're right, Alan; God has this, and all we have to do is give it to him and pray. I had better get to the station. Are you staying here or going to the church?"

"I'm going to the church. Please call me if you hear anything more from Ms. Holt, or if someone else files a charge against me."

"You've got it."

Alan goes to his office with a heavy heart. He falls into his chair and opens the bottom drawer of the desk. For a long time, he kept a bottle of whiskey there, but it tempted him too much, so he poured it down the drain. He had forgotten about that and was now looking at an empty bottle, much like his life. He said, "How could I have emptied that bottle? It would soothe my pain, but then again, I would be devastated if I took a drink—or would I?"

"Good morning, Pastor Alan," said Corinne.

Alan is startled and quickly closes the drawer, hoping he had quit talking to himself before she came into the office.

"I heard about the press conference, and I am not surprised who filed the complaint. Are you?"

"No, I am not surprised, and I'm actually less upset than I thought I would be about the announcement. The earth is still revolving around the sun, and I am still on the earth. Yet I know it will be hard. When I stopped to get gas on the way in, the cashier didn't respond to my greeting but just glared at me."

Alan visits several people in the hospital and prays with them and their families. Most had not heard the news, though someone did mention it. He responds he is innocent and is confident a court will find in his favor.

A KIDNAPPING REVIVAL

He then visits folks living in assisted living and other personal-care homes. Some of these really tug at the heartstrings. Some cannot talk; some cannot walk; some cannot hear; others can do none of these things. The ones with no family members or friends to visit are eager to talk to someone, and Alan gladly listens with his heart.

One of the residents Alan visits is Mr. Reed, who thanks Alan for what he did for Larry. Father and son are reconciled, and both are saved.

When Alan returns to the church, Charles is working with Corinne on Vacation Bible School. Several members call about the press conference, with most of them expressing support for the pastor. Since Charles and Corinne have everything under control, Alan gathers his correspondence to take home when Gary calls.

"Alan, I'm down at the station. Mary Jo Holt filed a complaint against you."

Alan leans against the wall and says, "What's the official charge and what kind of penalty does it carry?"

"The charge is sexual assault in violation of criminal code section 93-01-78. It carries a maximum term of fifteen years and a fifty-thousand-dollar fine. Do not come to the station. The charge will have to be investigated."

Alan waits at the church. *What better place to hide when your world is crashing?* He calls Honcho and says, "Mary Jo has filed a charge against me. I could go to prison for fifteen years for something I did not do! For now, I'm waiting here at the church to see if there will be another accusation before the night is over."

He reaches out to his attorney, saying, "Nathan, this is Alan. Did you watch the news?"

"Yes. How are you?"

"Angry and upset, to be perfectly honest, and waiting to see what else will happen."

Back at the compound, Beth askes Honcho, "Why would Mary Jo Holt go to Alan's office?"

"Alan counseled Mary Jo and her husband, but David left her anyway. Though she tried to forgive him, as Alan no doubt counseled, I have heard he continued to have an affair or two.

"The charge that Alan assaulted Mary Jo is ridiculous. Alan would not have anything to do with any woman other than Anna, both because of his belief in God and because of his deep love for Anna. He would never even show the slightest interest in any other woman.

"Whoever is driving these accusations has underestimated Alan. I just hope we can get information on the monster who has Anna," said Honcho.

"I agree," said Beth. "I am surprised Alan does not know someone who could be a suspect, someone who had or has a thing for Anna. But it could have been years ago or something only in the mind of the individual. It could be someone who just wants to ruin Alan's life by taking everything away from him. Wait, turn that up; I think they are saying something about Alan."

"Yes," said Honcho. "They are saying the police should look at Alan as a possible suspect in the disappearance of Anna. That is insane. How could anyone think he would do anything to hurt his wife? Next they'll be saying that he set the fire to his home."

"That's what one of the reporters just said. Poor Alan! He must be about ready to lose it! I think I hear Riley."

Hank said, "Mary Jo, you did a good job. Continue cooperating with the police investigation."

A KIDNAPPING REVIVAL

After dismissing Mary Jo, Hank said to Jeff, "Get in touch with Mr. Benton about his trip to the police station next week. The accounting study should have convinced the old man. At least I hope so. Go see him tomorrow and tell him he will be going to the police on Tuesday of next week. Tell him I will meet him Tuesday morning at his house to get him ready and take him to the lawyer who will represent him."

"So, did we get our first payment?" asked Jeff.

"Yes, I checked my account this morning, and the payment is there. The second payment will be made next week, and we can split after that," said Hank.

"I hope Mary Jo can handle the coming police investigation," said Jeff. "It will get more difficult."

"We can leave the state once Mr. Benton makes his police report and we receive our second payment, so it won't matter to us whether she can handle it or not. She may withdraw the complaint, saying it is too emotionally draining or something like that. I'll be in touch on Tuesday."

"Nathan, it's me again," said Alan after the second broadcast had aired. "I'm sorry to bother you, but did you hear the reporters' questions of whether I had something to do with Anna's disappearance and the house burning? Can you believe it?"

"Yes, Alan, I just saw it a few minutes ago and thought of calling you."

Alan wishes for a drink but instead says, "I am angry! I am ready to go to jail! I do not care anymore!

"I hate to think what will happen when the other accusation comes out. What kind of motives will the press dream up then? It really tests one's faith and mettle, and I feel like I'm lacking in both of those right now."

"You're not lacking in anything, Alan. The enemy of our souls is coming at you with both barrels. God will strengthen you. You are not alone. God is with you, and you have many friends who will stand with you through it all."

"Thanks, Nathan, for preaching to me. God knows I need it. I guess I'll go home and watch the story unfold from there, as there isn't anything I can do besides pray."

On the way home, Alan pulls into the gas station to buy a six-pack. He gets out of the truck, and Pete Boland comes up, slaps him on the back, and says, "Alan, you know us boys don't believe a word that crazy woman is saying about you, you being a preacher and all. We ain't afraid to say so neither."

"Thanks, Pete. You do not know how much you just helped me. God bless you! How are the wife and kids?"

"They're all as mean as ever. I heard about your wife, Alan. I am sorry. We will be praying, but it may not do no good. I hadn't been living life like I should, and God ain't blind."

"Thank you, Pete. I just wish other people were as humble as you are. I appreciate your honesty and your prayers."

When he went into the store, Alan took a longing look at the beer but grabbed a Coke instead. Once again, God had intervened.

"Honcho, is my daddy coming home?"

"Yes, son, your daddy is on his way home now. He had some things to take care of, but he wants to see you! He thinks about you even when he is not here. He loves you."

"I know he loves me. He told me so. I love him too. Here he is!"

"Hello, Riley. Hello, Honcho."

"We were just talking about you."

"Are you going to read to me tonight, Daddy?"

"Yes, indeed. Do you have a book picked out?"

"No, I'll find one now."

"Alan," said Honcho, "how are you? We heard the latest spin on the situation. What a crock!"

"Yes, it is unfair, unprofessional, outrageous, and downright evil to say I kidnapped my own wife and burned my own house! Have you ever heard of such a thing?"

"They've been off in left field before, but this is unprecedented. They must know how reckless they are. Anything for a story seems to be the guiding principle, no matter what they do to somebody's reputation."

As Anna sits at the kitchen counter drinking her juice, she asks, "Is anything wrong, Mrs. Bosco? It seems like you are worried about something."

"It's nothing you can help me with, Anna, though it's nice of you to ask."

"I can't help you, Mrs. Bosco, but Jesus can, and he is ready to help you. He promises to listen and to answer your prayers. He can handle whatever is bothering you, and you will not be alone. Say yes, Mrs. Bosco."

"I want to say yes, but I'm not ready, Anna. I have to face this on my own."

"Mrs. Bosco, you don't have to face anything alone. That's my point."

Anna prays Mrs. Bosco will change her mind. She is her own worst enemy, Anna thought. She remembers her own upbringing where every day, no matter how bad, was a day filled with love. She wondered if God's love reigned in Mrs. Bosco's childhood.

"Mrs. Bosco, you've never told me about your childhood and where you grew up."

"Not now, Anna, but maybe we can talk about it sometime."

The next day, Alan is driving to the bank to get a bridge loan to help while he is waiting for his insurance payment. His church salary would be running out in less than three months, and investigating costs were going up fast. A truck is following too closely behind him. He accelerates slightly, and so does the truck. He slows down enough for the truck to pass, but the truck slows down too. Alan swerves off the road into the gas station; the truck accelerates and goes on by. Trembling and breathing hard, Alan sits in his truck for several minutes following the encounter. Maybe the kidnapper plans to have him killed so he can legally marry Anna.

The bank officer, Maxine Caldwell, gives him a stern look and resists giving him a loan. He is not surprised with all the accusations and rumors floating around. Alan mortgages the compound with trepidation. He will be devastated if he loses the property, and Gary would never speak to him again.

Alan goes to see his insurance agent about his insurance claim, hoping he will get a friendlier reception. His agent, Miles Comer, is not in, so he speaks with James Baldwyn. He sits down in front of Baldwyn's desk and comes right to the point. "So, Mr. Baldwyn, when can I expect to receive payment on my home insurance claim?"

"Mr. Livingston, I did some checking. The cause of the fire was arson, and they have not eliminated you as a possible suspect."

Alan scoffed and said, "Don't they know a man in the jail is charged with the arson? How can they in good faith believe I would do such a thing? Everything I owned was in that house."

"Unfortunately, the man refuses to say anything about the arson, pleading not guilty."

"But I was not around when the house was burned. I was

thirty minutes away teaching a Bible study at our compound. It is up in Tishomingo County, in the middle of the woods. There are quite a few folks who can testify I was there until I received the shocking news my house was on fire."

When Alan says this, he stands up, paces, and continues making the case. He does not waver and speaks with conviction. Pointing his finger, he says, "I had nothing to do with the fire, just like I had nothing to do with my wife's kidnapping. Someone is calling the shots, and it is not me or anyone I know. Ask them to expedite the investigation. I had to go to the bank for a loan. Why would I put myself into such a predicament?"

"I understand, and I believe you. I will see what I can do. Better yet, let me introduce you to my boss. He can do more than I can."

"Mr. Livingston, this is—"

"What on earth are you doing here, Barry Barnes? James, I have known Barry since we were in junior high. I had no idea you were here, much less the boss! How are you?"

"I am fine, Alan. Is James taking good care of you?"

"Mr. Barnes," said James, "I'm filling in for Miles. Mr. Livingston has questions about his claim on his house that burned last week. It's been determined the cause of the fire was arson, and Mr. Livingston is still a suspect."

"Still a suspect? They really think this man burned his own house. I know for a fact he did not, and I will be glad to go to bat for him. James, thank you for bringing this to my attention. Alan, come into my office, so we can get this worked out. James, get Alan's file." Alan sits in front of Barry's desk, checking out his impressive array of awards.

Looking at the file, Barry said, "Alan, I see that our investigator is waiting on the police investigator. I will call him and find out about the results of his investigation.

"Mr. Long, this is Barry Barnes. I have Alan Livingston in

my office, and we are trying to find out when he can expect to get his claim paid. What can you tell me?"

"I've been ready to turn this file over to the office, but the police investigator asked me to wait, saying he thought Mr. Livingston was possibly involved."

"Did the investigator say why he believes this? What's his name?"

Alan makes a mental note to ask Gary about Eddie Baker. Most of the police force show their support for Alan in the search for Anna. This guy is a mystery. He turns his attention back to Barry, who is saying, "Okay, Mr. Long, have you spoken to the man in jail for the arson?"

"No, but I know the man pled not guilty to the arson charge. Neither Mr. Livingston nor anyone else has been mentioned for the arson."

"So, from all the evidence we have to date, nothing points to Alan as guilty," said Barry.

"That's correct," said Mr. Long.

"Here's what we are going to do. Turn in your report with the conclusion that Mr. Livingston is innocent. If there is any heat, I will deal with it. James, have the secretary prepare a claim approval form and bring it to me to sign. Alan, I will send it to the head office, and they will sign off on it and cut you a check. That will take about a week to ten days."

Alan jumps up and says, "Wow, Barry, you are amazing! Thank you for straightening this out and, most of all, for believing me. You are in the minority. And thank you, too, James. Barry, give Mr. Long my thanks."

Alan thanks God every minute after his visit to the insurance company, and he heads home with the good news. He is rejoicing so much he does not see the truck behind him. But when he gets on the interstate, he notices the truck and takes the next exit. He pulls into the service station. As expected, when Alan leaves the highway, the truck does not hang around, but Alan does get the license plate number and makes sure to note the make and model of the truck.

He relaxes his hands on the steering wheel, takes a few deep breaths, and calls Gary, saying, "A truck followed me like before. This time I got the information."

"I'll get Georgette to run this through. It will not take long. I'll see you back at the compound in an hour or so."

Alan dreads getting on the road again, but he does not see the truck in his rearview mirror. There is not much traffic on the state road, even less on the county road, and none on the private road, from which he pulls into the gate of the compound. Honcho is waiting for him at the barn.

"Hello, Honcho. Where's the boy?"

"He's helping Beth and Esther make jelly."

"That brings back a memory. I 'helped' Aunt Esther years ago," Alan said, making quotation marks in the air. "I managed to get jelly everywhere—in my hair, all over my clothes, and on the cat and the dog, and so did Gary. I think he was even worse!"

"Gary's on his way, so we'll wait for him. We won't tell him the ladies are making jelly," Alan said as they settled in the big, plush chairs of the library.

Honcho said, "The new security guard hasn't shown up the past two days."

"What kind of truck does he drive?"

"I'll check."

"Hi, Gary. Guess what, guys? I ran into an old friend today who happens to be a bigwig at the insurance company and got my claim approved. This was right after I got a loan at the bank. So, if all goes well, I will receive the insurance money to pay off the loan in record time.

"But as you know, I was followed by a truck this morning on

my way to town and this afternoon on my way back. I lost the truck both times by pulling into Moore's service station."

Gary said, "They're working on the information you gave me, and they should have something soon."

Alan said, "You know, I thought earlier today that maybe this lunatic is going to kill me since I didn't divorce Anna. I wonder why he cares about legalities, given his propensity to commit crimes. At least he hasn't killed anyone we know about."

Honcho said, "Hmm, someone who is a stickler for rules—an attorney, a judge, or a preacher."

As he moves from his chair to stand against the table, Gary said, "Honcho, you've got a good point."

"Alan, Mac is researching your and Anna's background, and you can help. Look through yearbooks and whatever to see if you can find someone who might have something against you or Anna or both of you. If you do, let Mac and me know. We will get him or her under surveillance. Meanwhile, I will be thinking about it too, as I know most of your early contacts.

"I've got to get back to the station."

"Let's have lunch first," Alan said. "Then I'll go to the church and search as you suggest. I will have to call some of my colleagues because of the house fire. But I have enough on hand at the office to get a start. By the way, Gary, a policeman named Eddie Baker seems to have it in for me. What's his deal?"

"He's just trying to make trouble and get attention as a bad dude. Plus, he doesn't like me."

Honcho said, "I'll follow up on why our security guard missed work, and if he has anything to do with the kidnapping.

"Alan, I'll send Ralph Logan here with you in case the truck shows up again."

Ralph said, "I'll be, if you didn't mess things up trying to have your way with that fine-looking woman. I'm surprised at you, preacher, for doing that, especially with your wife being kidnapped and all."

"Ralph, if I weren't a preacher, I'd bust you up good!" Alan said as he clenched his fists. "I never touched that woman or even tried to touch her! She was never in my office without her husband! I love my wife too much! Plus, I answer to God!"

Alan makes it to the church alone without incident. Charles is at the church in Alan's office. Alan sticks his head in the door. Charles is sitting in Alan's chair, drinking Alan's favorite coffee. Feeling replaced, Alan still manages to smile and say, "Hello, Charles. How's it going?"

"Really well, Alan. You have a fine church here, and your secretary, Corinne, is great. We had about thirty-five children at VBS; we had seven children give their lives to Christ; and three children recommitted their lives. How are you with all the rumors and inuendo?"

"I'm counting my blessings, not my sorrows. God will work everything together for good. I came to do research."

"I guess you need to use your office, and I've got plenty to do at home."

CHAPTER 11

Four days elapse before Alan is back in the church office. He continues his search for someone suspicious in his past, looking through old files, until he is interrupted by a phone call. It is a reporter asking for his response to the charge against him for embezzling money from the church. Alan replies he will talk to the press later when he has time to process the new charge. Alan calls Nathan.

"Nathan, I have never touched the money of this church. Is there anything we can do?"

"Yes, I'll look into hiring an investigator to review the accounting."

"Well, I am staying here at the church for a while. I want my wife back, and I need to talk to God."

Alan is still tempted and must battle the urge to drink almost every day. Thinking he had defeated that demon, he finally admits to himself that he has not; his last nerve is shot. So, he calls his old AA sponsor from Meridian.

After speaking with Alan, Nathan receives a strange call from Charles Winters, whom Nathan had heard about from Alan.

"Mr. Horowitz, I am calling regarding a mutual friend, Alan Livingston. He may not be all he seems."

Nathan said, "I am surprised to hear that. I assumed you and I would be on the same page, supporting Alan. What made you change your mind?"

Charles said, "It's not so much what changed my mind as what made me not change my mind. I did not know Alan before I was the chairman of the conference where he spoke on Christian persecution.

"At the conference, he said he had to leave because his wife had been kidnapped. Some of the pastors said Alan talked about his wife leaving him, and he said he knew how to stop her.

"When it was reported to me Alan seemed to be coming apart, I worried about what he would do. So, I volunteered to help with his church, and I called him to offer my assistance. Alan told me Jason Stone disrupted his church. What I did not know at the time was Alan and Stone know each other. Alan contacted Stone and asked him to come to his church. Moreover, Alan told Stone he did not care how much the service was disrupted.

"I will not be surprised if evidence comes to light about Alan's role in all this. Doesn't it seem strange to you how much has happened to Alan? I have heard that he is an addict. Maybe he is under the influence, or maybe he is schizophrenic or psychotic. I am not a doctor. And I am not a lawyer either. Am I way off base?"

"I don't know if you are or not. I will not change my mind about Alan based on what you have said, Mr. Allen, but I appreciate your confiding in me and ask you to continue to do so if more information becomes known to you."

After hanging up, Nathan wondered aloud, *Is Charles somehow involved in setting Alan up for the kidnapping? Why would he? Why would Alan invite Jason Stone to disrupt his church?* He planned to check with Alan's brother, Gary.

Anna's stomach curdles as she watches Mrs. Bosco stir-fry their dinner. So often lately, the meals were healthy, but Anna wants ice cream.

She is regressing to her childhood food choices, and maybe she has other areas of regression too, as she is outside her comfort zone by about a thousand miles! She has no earthly friend other than Mrs. Bosco, who is difficult at best, an enemy at worst. Her heavenly father makes everything bearable and will see her through these difficult times. She cannot make it without him.

"Anna," said Mrs. Bosco, "are you going to eat your dinner?"

Anna pushes her chair back, stands up, and says, "Mrs. Bosco, I appreciate your cooking for me, but I am craving ice cream."

Mrs. Bosco fixed herself a plate of stir-fry and dug in, while Anna drank two glasses of milk and ate two bananas.

"It's okay. I will see about getting you some different food tomorrow. It will be easier on me if I don't have to cook."

Larry said, "You mean it? You will marry me? Oh, Molly, you make my heart sing! When shall we have the ceremony?"

"Larry, I want to spend my life with you, and I want to get married right away." Molly dances in a circle with joy and anticipation. "Maybe Louise and her family and George and his family can all come for the wedding. Along with our friends and your dad, we will have a nice little wedding party. I can't wait to tell your dad!"

"Dad, guess what? Molly and I are going to jump the broom, tie the knot—get married! I asked, and she agreed to make me the happiest man alive!"

"Congratulations! This makes me so happy. I pray you will have many happy years together! I know just the pastor to perform the ceremony."

"Me too. Alan will be excited for Molly and me. We've been going to Good News."

"Maybe Louise can come. Molly, do you have family to invite?"

"Yes, I have a brother, George Davis, and his wife, Mary, and their three children, Joseph, Daniel, and Elizabeth. They live in Louisiana. My parents are divorced, and I haven't heard from either of them for the last five years."

Honcho visits his derelict security guard. The rear door is unlocked, and Ricky is tied up in his basement and looks ready to expire. Honcho unties him, gives him water and something to eat, and then asks him what happened as he dresses.

Ricky said, "Someone was waiting for me when I got home from work. I did not see him, and he knocked me out cold. When I woke up, my uniform had been taken off, and I was tied up. My cell phone was in my uniform pocket, and I could not get loose, so I had no way to call or come in. I had about decided I was going to die in my underwear."

Honcho wants to laugh but instead pats Ricky's shoulder, saying, "You're a good man, and that's why I decided to make a house call when you didn't answer your phone. Did you see the man who knocked you out?"

"No, or I would have knocked him out! I didn't see his face, and the only thing I noticed about him is he is shorter than me."

Honcho calls the security room at the compound and tells them to be on the lookout for someone wearing the stolen security guard uniform.

Erring on the side of caution, Honcho assumes there is a connection between the theft of the uniform and the kidnapping. Someone in the compound is a likely target.

Gary arrives at the station to question Gene Rogers, the driver of the truck that followed Alan. He denies doing anything, saying Alan is imagining things.

"How do you know Alan?"

"Everyone around here knows Alan, especially now that he's in the news so much."

"Who hired you to torment Alan?"

"If you're going to question me like a criminal, I want a lawyer, and I want to make a phone call."

Gary charges the man with reckless driving and calls Billy to check the truck for prints. As they know already, whoever is directing the kidnapping is careful. The only thing they find about the truck is its owner.

"Hello, Honcho, this is Gary. We have been dealing with the driver who followed Alan. We charged him with reckless driving. How did your search for the security guard go?"

"He was knocked out by someone who stole his uniform. I am back at the compound now. There have been no incidents involving the stolen uniform or other disturbance. All is quiet."

"I'll get Billy to check out the security guard's house."

"Beth," said Esther as she entered the kitchen, "did you ever talk with Mrs. Livingston about the memoirs her husband was writing?"

They got coffee and sausage biscuits and sat down at the bar. Then Beth said, "No, I didn't know he was writing his memoirs. Gary and I were only married five years before their accident. Mrs. Livingston seemed to be a very proper and sweet lady. Mr. Livingston seemed stand-offish, but I reminded myself he was a research scientist. I am surprised he wrote memoirs."

Esther stands up to turn off the stove and says, "Mrs. Livingston was good to Manny and me. Her trust in God inspired us. Mr. Livingston did not know how to deal with us. Manny and I practically raised Gary and Alan.

"Back to the present. We can look for the memoirs and other papers. Gary said maybe the older Livingstons did something to cause the kidnapping and arson. I wonder, though, why you and Gary are not also targets if the parents did something untoward."

"That's kind of scary," said Beth.

Esther continues, saying, "The papers are in boxes in a temperature-controlled storage room, labeled by author and year. There are many of them written by Dr. Livingston. She did some writing too, though not as much as he did. I think Gary and Alan will be glad for us to look through the boxes. Who knows? Maybe we can solve the case!"

Beth was not convinced the search would solve the kidnapping, but any hope it gave made it worth doing. She looked out the kitchen window at Manny and Riley and felt the familiar pang.

"Dear Alan," she writes, "you may never see this, but I am believing you will because we serve an awesome God who loves us more than we could ever imagine. I want you to know how much I love you and Riley and how much I miss you.

"Oh, Alan, I think of you all hours of the day and night and look forward to our reunion. It is hard being away from you, and I know Riley is growing, and I am missing it. But to end this letter on a high note, you are my heart. You are the exclamation point at the end of my sentences. You are the whipped cream and dark chocolate syrup on my sundae. You are the high note in my song. You are the colors of the rainbow. You are the sound of thunder, the light of lightning, and the coolness of the rain. May God keep us together through this period of separation. May he forgive my times of despair. All my love forever, Anna."

When she finishes her letter, she places it in the folder with the others. Then she joins Mrs. Bosco in the small living room, which has no windows, like the other rooms in the small house. She said, "Mrs. Bosco, I will look back over this time with you as time well spent if you become a child of the King of kings. Can't I interest you in considering Jesus as your Lord and Savior by pleading with you one more time? It is the most important decision of your life because it determines where you will spend eternity and how you spend your remaining days on the earth. Instead of being alone, you will always have the Lord with you. Instead of fear and anxiety, you will have faith, love, joy, and peace. Being a Christian is the best thing that ever happened to me, and I want the best for you, Mrs. Bosco."

"Anna, you've convinced me God is real; he loves you; and he takes care of you. Your lack of fear makes me understand how much Jesus means to you. I do want that kind of love and peace, but I do not think I can give him my life. Do you understand what I mean?"

"Yes, I think I do. I think you are not free to make decisions disagreeing with someone who has authority over you. I will pray for your freedom. You can ask Jesus to deliver you. There is nothing too hard for Him. You will see his power in your life, Mrs. Bosco, if you ask him. He is a miracle-working God."

Anna returns to her room as Mrs. Bosco goes to the kitchen to check on the supply of ice cream. Anna lies back on her bed, reading a book Mrs. Bosco found for her.

―――∽∾∽―――

This day is better for Alan than most. He receives a check from the insurance company and goes to the bank and then to the church.

"Good morning, Pastor Alan," said Charles when Alan comes to his office door. "What are you up to this morning?"

"Good morning," said Alan as he takes in the changes Charles made to his office, with his plaques and pictures. He stands at the door and says, "I must have been on autopilot. After I went to the bank, I came here."

"I'm going over my sermon notes for Sunday. Do you plan to be here? I have not found a replacement pianist for Beth. I didn't expect them to take time off just because you are on leave."

"You'll have to talk to them about that."

"I will. I am glad you came by. The other pastors and I have not found anything about Jason Stone. Have you learned anything about him?"

"No, except he works at a local auto-repair shop. Maybe I should talk with him. In fact, I think I will. Maybe I can get some answers."

"That is not a good idea, Alan. Stone is a loose cannon. It will not be safe for you to confront him. I advise you not to go."

"I've played it too safe too long. It's time to get in the game."

"Mr. Stone," said Alan, as he arrives at the auto-repair shop, "I am Alan Livingston, and I want to see if we can make peace. I agree with much of what you said in my church. I would like to see if I can make amends to you for whatever made you try to scare my church members away."

Stone looks shocked and steps away from Alan as they make their way to the side of the shop. They must step around a pile of old tires. Stone does not say anything for a few minutes and keeps his eyes glued to the ground. Finally, he says, "Your parents went to my daddy's church, the same church where you preach. They caused the congregation to throw my daddy, my momma, and me out on the street. My daddy was ruined and had to leave the ministry altogether. My momma was shamed and lost all her friends. I was bullied and made fun of at school."

Pointing his greasy finger at Alan, he moved closer and said,

"We had to move away, and the only work my daddy could find was in a factory about fifty miles from here. I came back. I was going to get my revenge against your parents, but before I could get to them, somebody else did. That leaves you and your brother. A policeman is hard to get to, but you and your church are easy pickings. I did not even have to break any laws. God is on my side. Your parents are killed; your wife is kidnapped; your house is burned; and you lost your church. What better revenge could there be?"

Alan moves back a bit but keeps his eyes focused on Stone's eyes. He said, "You know the scriptures where God said, 'Vengeance is mine,' and where Jesus tells us to 'turn the other cheek.' But I'm not here to preach you a sermon."

"You'd better not be preaching to me. I have heard all your preaching I care to hear. You may think I study the Bible, and I did before my family was ruined by your family. Your family not only ruined our lives down here on earth, they tried to take heaven from us too. That did not happen to my parents, but it did to me. I have nothing for God anymore," said Stone.

"I have been told the reason my parents wanted the church to fire your father was because he preached against Jews and Catholics," said Alan.

"My daddy never did anything but love your daddy and momma, and they were repaid by getting everything taken away from them. You can talk about revenge all you want, but I bet you would feel the same way. You know you want revenge against the kidnapper, if you are honest with yourself, preacher or not."

"You may be right, but I try to pray for the kidnapper as Jesus taught us to do. I ask you to forgive my parents. Just as it is human to want to seek revenge, it is also human to make mistakes. I know my parents' mistake may have ruined your life, but I plead for your forgiveness.

"I will pray for you, Mr. Stone. Maybe someday we can talk peaceably, and forgiveness will be in our hearts. Do not forget how precious you are to God. Bad things happen to good people but not because God does not love us. We live in a fallen world. God bless you, Mr. Stone. If you ever want to talk, you know where to find me, and you are welcome anytime."

"You don't want me to find you, preacher," Stone says as he jerks himself around and stomps back to the shop.

Alan stands still for several minutes after he disappears, thinking Jason Stone had experienced much hate and much pain. Maybe Alan's parents could have handled the situation better. He prays for Stone and knows it will not be the last time.

The compound is buzzing when Alan arrives. Beth and Esther are in the storage area looking through his parents' papers. Riley is with Manny. Honcho has returned to the compound from the security guard's house. Gary is still at the station dealing with the truck driver.

"Alan," said Honcho, "did you hear about our security guard's ordeal?"

"No. Why don't you fill me in on that, Honcho. I want to hold off on my news until Gary gets home. Gary probably already knows about the security guard, right?"

"Yes, I told him earlier."

"By the way, what is the man's name?"

"His name is Ricky Rivers. Here is how it went down."

About the time Honcho finishes telling Alan about Ricky's ordeal, Riley dashes into the room and grabs his dad around his legs. Alan reaches down and picks Riley up, hugging him back.

Gary arrives right behind Riley, and they have an early dinner. Manny says the blessing, and they feast on chicken and dumplings, baby lima beans, summer squash, coleslaw, cornbread, iced tea or lemonade, and iron skillet apple pie with homemade vanilla ice cream for dessert.

As he rises from the dinner table, Alan says, "It's a miracle you guys aren't huge! I have never eaten so well as I have since being here. Beth and Esther, you are wonderful cooks. Thank you!

"Riley," said Alan, "you help Aunt Beth and Aunt Esther wash dishes and clean up the kitchen. Then they will help get your bath. You be good and do what they tell you."

The men sit across from each other at a table in the security office. Alan said, "I visited Jason Stone today. He said he tried to scare our church members because our parents ruined the lives of his family. I told him our parents were involved in firing his father because of his father's hatred of Jews and Catholics.

"He moved back here to take our parents out, but someone else got to them first, he said. He also said he did not kidnap Anna or set the fire.

"Apparently he believes our parents were murdered. Maybe after all this is over, you can investigate their accident."

"Wow," said Gary. "The man must have really hated our parents and, by association, hates us as well.

"As to the truck driver who tried to run you off the road, we ran the prints, and the driver is who he said he is, Gene Rogers. The name of the owner of the truck is Maxine Caldwell, the banker. Didn't she approve your loan?"

"Yes, she did not want to, but she did. You say she owns the truck the man was driving and trying to run me off the road or at least scare me?"

"Yes," said Gary. "I wonder what her motive would be. I'll look into that and whether the truck is stolen or if there is some other explanation for her truck being used against you."

Honcho said, "I can't believe Maxine had anything to do with this. I dated her back in the day before she married that Caldwell fellow."

"Yeah, I am with Honcho. Maxine wouldn't try to scare me," said Alan. "Who knocked out Ricky and stole his uniform?"

"No idea," said Gary.

As they retired to their quarters, Gary and Beth had time together alone when they were not exhausted.

Gary said, "The case seems to be heating up. How about you, hon?"

"Oh, Gary, you do know how to sweet-talk a girl. How about some more ice cream?"

"You know my weaknesses, Elizabeth! Sure, I am for ice cream if you will join me. We can have it in bed."

"Now that's smooth, big guy! I'll get our ice cream and meet you there."

The next day, Hank and Jeff, the handlers of the accusers, talk about their work as they drink the last of their coffee from the motel. Jeff asks Hank, "Did we get our last payment after Mr. Benton did his thing?"

"I got mine," said Hank. "You'll have to check your account to see if you got yours. The boss has another job for us if you are up to it. It's more to do with Alan Livingston, as you might guess," said Hank.

"What does he have in mind?"

"I don't know. He just wants to know if he can count on us."

"I thought we were going to vanish after we were paid for taking care of the two accusers," said Jeff, thinking he is too dependent on Hank.

"You can do that. If that is what you want, go for it."

The next morning, Gary goes to the bank to meet with Maxine Caldwell. "Ms. Caldwell, I'm Detective Gary Livingston. I'd like to ask you a few questions." Gary does not sit until Maxine motions him to a chair in front of her desk.

"Am I in trouble, Detective Livingston?"

"It depends, Ms. Caldwell, and I can't answer your question until you answer some of mine. Shall I begin?"

"Yes, I suppose. Go ahead. Would you like some coffee?"

"No, thank you," said Gary as he took the chair in front of her desk. "I would like to ask if you own a 1996 green Chevrolet Sierra truck."

"Yes, I do."

"Who drives this truck?"

Ms. Caldwell continues to hold out her hands to look at her nails and says, "My nephew, Gene Rogers, and my niece, Jean Rogers."

"When was the last time your niece or nephew drove your truck?"

"I'm not sure," said Ms. Caldwell as she applied lipstick while looking in her small hand mirror. "I don't use it except when I need to haul something on the weekends, so it's available to them through the week. They have keys, and I have a key."

"Do you know my brother, Alan Livingston?"

"Yes. I recently approved a loan for him. Did you know he mortgaged your property to get the loan?"

"I'm asking the questions," Gary said gruffly as he recalled signing something for Alan without reading it, for he trusted his little brother.

"What does your nephew do for a living?"

"Gene? I do not know what he is doing, maybe nothing. My brother pays his bills when he's out of work."

"Do you know where your nephew was over the past two days?"

"No."

"Your nephew was charged with reckless driving last night. He tried to scare Alan off the road. I would advise you to take the key back from Gene and let him get his own ride. The truck is at the station."

"Thank you, Detective Livingston. I apologize for Gene's behavior. I have no idea why he did such a thing."

"Thank you, Ms. Caldwell, for speaking to me this morning. I will let you get back to work."

"It was a pleasure to meet you, Detective Livingston."

Gary said, "Honcho, the Memphis police brought Roger Cutlow in for questioning on an unrelated matter and noticed our interest. We now have his address, phone number, and employer information. I've put in a call to a friend on the Memphis force."

"Good," said Honcho. "Alan has taken about all he can, but God is in control, and Anna is okay. That is an important difference between this kidnapping and most kidnappings.

Molly is thanking God and dancing and twirling. Her brother and his family are coming. Larry's sister and her family are coming. Larry arranges for Pastor Alan to conduct the ceremony. Beth is doing the music. Beth and Esther are taking care of the decorations and the refreshments.

Having never been around people so giving, Molly realizes Jesus makes all the difference.

"Larry, can you believe this time next week we will be Mr. and Mrs. Lawrence Reed?'

"Yes, my sweet Molly," Larry said as he grabs her hand and dances with her.

CHAPTER 12

"Pastor Alan, I need to talk with you privately," said Mr. Benton.

"Sure, we will go into the adult Sunday school room since Charles is using the office and Corinne is out front. We'll have privacy there."

"Don't tell anybody what I tell you, please! I don't want to interfere with your search for Anna, but my grandson's life may depend on your silence." Benton's anguish showed on his face and his voice resonated with sincerity.

"About three weeks ago, a man named Hank contacted me and asked if I valued the life of my grandson, Michael. You can imagine my outrage at such a question and my response. The man then told me Michael would be murdered if I did not bring a charge of embezzlement against you."

Benton lets out a long breath, as though feeling a sense of freedom from breaking his silence and sharing his burden.

Benton continues, "At first, I resisted. I told them you were the most honest man I had ever known. But the man said he had proof you embezzled money from the building fund. Hank's partner, Jeff, brought me an accounting report showing you had taken money from the church on a regular basis.

"Given the proof and the dire threat, I went through with the accusation even though I felt like I had dirty hands," Benton said as he rubbed his hands together. "Please forgive me even though I don't deserve it. I do not deserve forgiveness from God either. I would give my life for my grandson, but I had no right to ruin yours."

Alan looks straight into the man's eyes, and says, "Mr. Benton, I am so sorry you have been used and abused in this manner. Of course, I forgive you. I will not betray your confidence, no matter the cost. The consequence of talking is too horrible even to consider. I understand, and if you agree, I will tell only my brother, who will keep your confidence."

Benton relaxes his hands, sits back in his chair, and says, "Yes, Pastor. I do not mind your telling your brother, and I appreciate your promise to keep my confidence, so my grandchild will be safe.

"The man who talked with me is probably not the kidnapper, nor is his partner. They struck me as men just doing their jobs without much thought about the morality of their actions. And that's about all I can tell you."

"Well, Gary can help you remember things you don't know you know. But I cannot tell you how much I appreciate you. I thought the day you were in the sanctuary you really wanted to talk, and I wondered why you did not. Now I know. Thank you for coming to me. God bless you and your family, especially your grandson Michael. Where do they live?"

"My daughter and her husband and their four children live in Florida. Michael is the youngest and the only boy. They will be visiting sometime this fall. I'll be sure to let you know so you can meet them."

"Thanks. I will enjoy meeting them, and Michael is on my prayer list as of today. I will talk to you on Sunday. You will be coming back to church, won't you?"

"I'm not sure I'd be welcome, and my wife needs me. I'll wait until Anna comes home."

Once he arrives back at the compound, Alan loses no time in retelling Mr. Benton's story privately to Gary in the library, after securing Gary's promise to keep it quiet. The two discuss the sad story.

Alan said, "Mr. Benton said he felt like he had dirty hands, so he must have suspected the evidence he was given to prove the embezzling was false.

"Unfortunately, you cannot share his testimony with anyone, and you'll have to continue letting folks think you're a criminal," said Gary.

"Gary, it's more than worth it to keep Mr. Benton's grandson, Michael, alive. I would never consider doing otherwise. I wonder about Mary Jo. She had her own reasons to get back at me, but I don't think she would have falsely accused me if the life of a person important to her had not been at risk."

"Alan, there is a person who is orchestrating all these things and using people to accomplish what he wants. If he cannot get them through one means, he tries another. I am not sure he would carry out the threatened murders, but it is too big of a chance to take.

"By the way, when were you going to tell me you mortgaged the compound? I cannot believe you did that. I am sure you could have gotten a loan somewhere else. Why on earth would you risk our home?"

"Don't you think Anna is worth it?"

"Just because you can't handle money without her help is no reason to mortgage the compound."

Gary enjoys a late breakfast before going to Nathan's office. For the first day in quite a while, he has time for a second cup of coffee and time to read his Bible. He usually reads at night, but it is special to start a day with the Word of God.

"Good morning, Gary. I'm glad you could come," said Nathan, gesturing toward a seat in front of his desk. "I have an issue involving your brother. Do you know Charles Winters?"

"No, I know only that he is preaching for Alan while he is on leave."

Nathan said, "He told me about what Alan supposedly said to other pastors in Atlanta. He also said Alan and Jason Stone are friends, and Alan approved Stone's idea of disrupting the church. He mentioned that Stone visited other churches besides Good News."

Gary said, "Alan told me about meeting with Jason Stone. He did not know Stone, and the accusation that Alan condoned scaring the church members is ludicrous.

"Our parents are the people who ran Stone's parents out of town, according to Stone. He moved back here to avenge his parents, but when our parents died, he was left with only Alan and me."

Nathan said, "Do you have any idea why Charles would act like such a good friend to your brother but lie to him? Why would he try to turn me against Alan? Does he have his own agenda or is he working with the kidnapper? Is he the kidnapper?"

"Mrs. Bosco, I think I may be pregnant. Would you get me an at-home pregnancy test?"

Mrs. Bosco looks up from reading her magazine and said, "Yes, I will. Maybe that is why your appetite has changed. You have asked for ice cream. How about pickles?"

"Not yet," said Anna with a smile.

"Were you and your husband trying to get pregnant?"

"We weren't trying to get pregnant, but we weren't trying not to get pregnant either. We hope to have a little brother or sister for our son. It will be an answer to prayer if I am pregnant, although the timing is not ideal."

Anna retires to her corner of the small living room and writes to Alan and Riley and her dad. Her letter to Alan says she might be pregnant. "I see you on the other side of my bed, kissing me with intense passion and gently caressing my growing belly."

Alan cannot resist stopping by the church even though he is on leave. Nonetheless, he sticks his head in to check on things. Charles is not in, so Alan goes into his old office to see if he can find information on his associates. While looking, Alan sees a note sticking out of a pile of papers on the credenza, with Jason Stone's name on it. Alan carefully removes the note and, upon hearing a noise, crams it into his pocket and leaves the office in a hurry. As he is walking away, Corinne calls out.

"Don't be in such a hurry. Charles is out for the day with a cold or the flu. You are welcome to spend some time with me. I'll catch you up on what you've been missing."

"Thanks, Corinne, but I'd better be off. I will take you up on that later. Maybe you can come out to dinner at the compound soon. The ladies would love to see you."

Alan waits until he is back at the compound to read the note. He pulls it out of his pocket. The note said, "Jason Stone new number 891-2547/next job Livingston place." Alan ponders what the note means. The note was in Charles's office. Did that mean Charles and Stone were working together? Did it mean Charles and Stone were involved in the kidnapping? He calls Gary and Honcho.

Gary arrives and says, "Okay, little brother, what do you have?

Before we start, I need to tell you I'm sorry about what I said last night."

"I forgive you. Even if I did not like what you said, I will get over it."

"Here's what I wanted to show you. What do you think it means?"

"Where did you come up with this?"

"I found it in a stack of papers in my old office. Neither Corinne nor Charles was there. Of course, I about lost it when I heard someone come in."

"Maybe you could talk with Corinne and see if she will replace it for you and, at the same time, look for more. We'll meet with Honcho when he and Beth get back with Riley."

"Corinne, I need to speak with you privately and confidentially. Most of all, I must ask that you not speak to Charles about what I say. Can you do that?"

"Yes, I know you wouldn't ask me if it didn't involve something important. I won't say anything to Brother Charles or anyone else."

"Good. First, here is a note I found this morning. I was looking for yearbooks and other information for the case when I happened to look down and see this sticking out of a stack of papers."

"What is the note talking about?"

"I don't know exactly. It seems Charles and Jason are working together and talking about the compound. Would you look to see if there are other notes like this one?"

"He does most of his own typing. I do not see what he writes—notes, sermons, and the like. I answer the phone and type the bulletin. I can look right now. Do you want me to put the note back in the stack?"

"Yes, replace it so that he will not know we are on to him. See if there are any others."

Corinne spends a few minutes going through the stack and then said, "I don't see any others, but I'll check again in a few days."

"Be careful. We don't know how he might react."

"I'll be careful, and you be careful too. You're the one with the target drawn on his back."

"Why don't you come to dinner tonight if you don't have other plans."

"Right now, I don't have any plans, and if Rory calls, I'll make our date for tomorrow night."

"Rory? You could bring him with you."

"I'm not ready to bring him, but I will if I think he is the one. He will have to get your seal of approval."

Alan calls Honcho as he drives back to the compound.

"Honcho, did Gary fill you in?"

"Yes, he did. How are you?"

"I'm fine. Maybe Charles Winters or Jason Stone punched out your security guard and took his uniform. That would go along with the note about getting into the compound."

"Yes, it would, Alan. Looks like Gary isn't the only one with law enforcement instincts in the family."

"Don't be too impressed."

"Where's Riley?"

"Taking a nap. Beth may be taking a nap with him. Esther is in the kitchen."

Esther is cooking when Alan goes into the kitchen. "Hi, Aunt Esther. How are you? I invited Corinne to dinner tonight. I hope that is okay."

"Yay. She is still working for you?"

"Yes. She is a treasure."

"Someone told me you and Beth are going through my parents' papers. Have you found anything related to the investigation?"

"No, we haven't found anything yet, but Manny and I were here when the problems with Stone were going on."

"Why, of course. How dumb of me not to think of that before. What do you and Manny remember about it?"

"Pastor Stone was a good speaker and had many followers, including your parents and Manny and me. After about three years though, he started preaching against Jews and Catholics. It just came out of nowhere! We could never figure out what turned him against the Jews and the Catholics."

"Do you remember his son?"

"Oh, yes, he was a precious little boy, not real bright but super sweet. He was a few years older than Gary. You were just a baby when they left."

"Did my parents actually run the preacher off?"

"They headed up the committee that recommended his firing. Your parents were blessed with many Jewish friends and some Catholic friends. It was the attack on God's chosen people that caused the most consternation. They could not tolerate a supposed man of God who spewed hate.

"It was suggested that maybe Brother Stone had a stroke or other physical or psychological illness that caused the change in his theology. 'Still,' said your parents, 'no matter what the cause, the Stones have to go.' I really felt sorry for Mrs. Stone and their young son, but Brother Stone claimed he was the victim of Christian persecution, even though Christians were the ones who fired him. He would not recant his cruel and bitter criticism."

"Were any other remedies pursued?"

"No, Alan, firing him was the only option. Manny and I completely agreed with your parents."

"Thank you for telling me this, Aunt Esther. If you find

anything about this or anything that could be a motive for Anna's kidnapping, I know you will tell us immediately. Gary will be investigating our parents' accident later as a possible homicide. By the way, I am glad you and Beth are working on the papers. I'm sure Riley is enjoying his time with Uncle Manny."

"No more than Manny is enjoying his time with that precious boy!"

"Speaking of whom. Hello, Riley! How's my boy?"

"I been having fun with Uncle Manny. He funny. Want to see the puppies?"

"Sure, I bet those puppies are growing. Lead the way."

After dinner with Corinne, Gary and Alan moved to the library, while Corinne visited with the others.

"I'm just wondering, Alan, when we'll hear from the kidnapper. You refused to give in to his demands. What's his next move?"

"Gary, I don't have a clue. More questions than answers."

"You've got that right. Honcho told me your idea about the attack against the security guard. Seems to fit. Good call.

"Do we know anyone who works with Charles Winters or Jason Stone? I know you said Corinne will look for future notes, but I wonder if there is anyone who can watch these men," said Gary.

"I cannot believe how much Charles Winters has lied to me. How could I have been so deceived? I think he has deceived many others besides me. God is in control, though, so these evil schemes have no chance of ultimate success," said Alan.

CHAPTER 13

Anna is on the floor of the living room exercising. Mrs. Bosco is on the couch. Anna said, "Mrs. Bosco, the test says I'm pregnant. I guess that explains my craving for ice cream. I wish I could tell my husband. He will be thrilled, and so will my son. When will I get to go home, Mrs. Bosco?"

"I don't know anything about the future, Anna. No one confides in me. I'm as clueless as you are."

Finishing her push-ups and lying on the floor trying to catch her breath, Anna said, "There are things I will need, prenatal vitamins for a start, to go along with the ice cream. This all seems so surreal that I am pregnant away from my husband and son. Please ask your boss to let me go. I promise nothing will ever happen to any of you if you'll just let me go home."

"I'd let you go if I could, Anna. I have come to care for you, and I want to know your God before you go anywhere. Will you tell me more about your God now?"

"Yes, of course. Nothing would make me happier than for you to become a child of God. We can never be good enough on our own to come into God's presence. Only through the death of Jesus are we allowed to be reconciled to God. He died for you. Do you want Jesus to forgive you of your sins and become your Lord and Savior?

"If you do, just tell him you are sorry for your sins and you want him to save you and be the Lord of your life. You can talk to him anytime. Even if you cannot talk out loud sometimes, he can hear your thoughts. He loves you so much. He will never let you go once you give your life over to him. Do you want to pray now?"

"Yes, yes, I want to pray. Dear Jesus, I have been so wrong and have done so much wrong. I ask you to forgive me and take me in and be my Lord and Savior. Oh, Lord, I want you to be with me always. I want to do you proud. Thank you for loving me. Amen," she said, as she wiped the tears from her eyes.

"And thank you for loving me and praying for me, Anna."

"Welcome to the family of God! We are sisters in the Lord and will spend all eternity together. I am so excited for you! Do you mind if I give you a hug?"

"Of course not," she said as she hugs Anna. "You have made this the most wonderful day in my life, Anna. Thank you."

"It's the Lord, not me, but I am glad he let me have a small part. I do have a question for you. What is your first name, if you do not mind telling me? I have always called you Mrs. Bosco and have never known your full name."

"Yes, of course, my name is Maria, and from now on, I want you to call me Maria."

"What a beautiful name!"

"Thank you. It was my mother's name. I miss her so much."

"I miss my mother too. Good night, Maria. Sleep tight and don't let the bedbugs bite." Seeing Maria's confused expression, Anna explains, "As a little girl, I heard this saying right before bedtime every night from my granddaddy."

Laughing, Maria said, "Good night, Anna. Thank you again."

"Just continue to talk to God and listen to what he has to say in his Word, the Bible, and in your heart. You must have a Bible. You need to read it every day and pray every day. Make sure you get one when you make out the shopping list. In the meantime, use mine. I would suggest starting with the book of Luke."

The next evening, after the compound residents settle in for dinner and Riley says the blessing, Beth said, "Saturday is wedding day for Larry and Molly."

"What time?"

"It's at two o'clock. Alan, you will need to wear a tux. Do you have one, or do you want to borrow Gary's? I assume yours burned up."

"Yes, may I borrow yours, Gary, if it fits? Anything else I need to know, Beth?"

"Are you meeting with the bride and groom before their wedding day? Maybe meet with them on Thursday. Their families will be here tomorrow, and we can invite them all for dinner on Thursday night if you men will grill burgers. Esther and I will fix the side dishes, trimmings, and dessert, something with homemade ice cream, which you men can also fix."

"That's a great idea, Beth," said Alan. "I'll meet with them Thursday afternoon, and then everyone will have dinner here Thursday night. If everyone agrees, I'll give Larry a call after dinner."

Gary said, "Mr. Benton, thank you for letting me come see you. As I explained on the phone, I am Detective Gary Livingston, Alan's brother, and the local investigating officer on the kidnapping case."

"Come in and have a seat in the kitchen. It's my office."

"Thank you. I would like to ask you a few questions. Alan explained to me the need to keep quiet about this, and I assure you that we will.

"Do you remember the person who outlined the accusation and threat to you?"

"Yes. He was tall, about your height and about your weight. He had brown hair worn in a ponytail. His skin was light brown, and his eyes were dark brown, almost black. He was wearing jeans, a cowboy shirt tucked in, and cowboy boots. He was friendly but had a cruel look on his face, and his eyes chilled you to the bone. I had no doubt he would not have minded, and might even have enjoyed, carrying out the threat to my grandson. I did not cross him."

"Did he have an accent?"

"Not unless you count a southern drawl."

"Ha. So, he sounded local then?"

"Yes, sir, except he might have been faking it."

"You would know if he was faking, your being southern and all," said Gary with his best southern accent.

"Did he have any distinctive smells? Did he speak anyone's name in his conversation? Did he seem at ease when he spoke to you?"

"He smelled like cigarettes. He mentioned his partner, whose name was Jeff, and he seemed at ease when he spoke to me. I can't think of anything else."

"Corinne," said Charles on the phone, "I am still ill and may not be able to preach on Sunday. Is there someone who can pinch hit?"

"I suppose Alan could."

"Well, that might go against the policy of the board. We should find someone else."

"I can't think of anyone else."

"I'll just have to get well by Sunday, I guess."

"God is our healer."

"Are you ready for tomorrow night's big bash, my sweet Elizabeth?"

"Yes, Gary, my main man, I am as ready as I can be."

"I'm sure it will be great! Then you have the wedding on Saturday. You will be exhausted. Maybe I can take off work and take you on a short vacation."

"That would be wonderful," said Beth.

"Come on over here a little closer and tell me how wonderful," said Gary as he pulled Beth over to his side.

"I don't know how you make everything sound so sexy, but I like it," said Beth as she put her arms around Gary's neck and kissed him. She then switched off the lamp.

"Molly and Larry," said Alan, at the church in the sanctuary, "I feel so close to God when I come here. May our words be pleasing to him."

"Thank you for meeting with us, Pastor Alan. You have been such a blessing to us and to my dad," said Larry.

"You are welcome. I am glad to have the opportunity to meet with you. I want to go over the Word of God as it speaks to marriage between a man and woman and how they relate to each other and to God. I will start by saying a family is blessed by the joint prayers of the husband and wife. Turn to the fifth chapter of Ephesians."

"Larry," said Molly, "I want to introduce you to my brother, George Davis, his wife, Mary, and their sons, Daniel and Joseph, and their daughter, Elizabeth. And this is my fiancé, Larry."

"Molly, you've met Louise. This is Louise's husband, Seth Marks, and their two daughters, Susan and Marilyn. And you can all introduce yourselves to each other. We are being treated to a cookout tonight for family and friends."

"Well, now that everybody knows everybody else," said Alan, "make yourselves at home. Kids, there are board games inside and ballgames outside. Your coach is Grandpa Jon. I am turning the group over to you, Dad. Let him know what you want to play."

"All right, kiddos," said Jon. "Pick outside or inside. Let me see your hands. Outside, inside. Outside wins." The kids all jump up to go outside.

"Come on, Riley. Here are the puppies." The kids tumble over one another petting the puppies and picking them up.

The next day, Larry and Molly say their vows, and the folks are treated to cake and other goodies.

As Alan, Gary, and Manny help Beth and Aunt Esther take down the decorations and clean, they hear an explosion. Running outside, they do not get there in time to see Alan's truck explode, but they could see the aftermath, which included a young man bleeding from his head, a young woman's arm bleeding, and an older man's leg bleeding. The injuries were all minor, as the truck was parked behind the church, and the folks had been departing from the front.

Beth and Esther help the injured, and Alan and Gary run to the back to see the truck. Gary calls the explosion in.

"This is just more of the same," Alan said. "You would think they would give up after a while. Why do they want to torture me? What have I ever done to them?"

The police arrive. The injured go to a nearby clinic. None of the injuries is a problem, though Mr. Reed's leg is given special consideration due to his age and medical issues. Larry and Molly are on their way to Florida for their honeymoon.

Alan visits Mr. Reed while Gary and the police check out the truck. "Mr. Reed," said Alan, "I was happy to see your son marry Molly today. I know you are proud of him."

"I appreciate your forgiving him and leading him to Jesus. He then led me to Jesus. I have high hopes for him and his sweet bride, Molly."

CHAPTER 14

Hank and Jeff are proud of themselves for exploding the truck. Hank is somewhat disappointed there are no casualties, but their boss wants only to torment and dishearten, not kill. Their accounts are fatter today than they were yesterday.

Exploding the truck is child's play compared to the arson they did along with Jim Boren. He was the lookout—more of a hindrance, thinks Hank, and Hank thinks the same about Jeff.

Whether to go or stay? That is the question facing the two men. Jeff wants to leave, but Hank always wants more mayhem and money. Many scenarios need two men instead of one, so Hank convinces Jeff to stay.

Gary simply cannot leave. Beth understands, even though she is a disappointed. Riley always makes her smile, and Esther is a balm to her soul. So, why is she upset Gary cannot take time off?

Beth and Esther continue to go through the papers of the elder Livingstons. Their workspace keeps the papers organized and the women comfortable. They find information about the church. The memoirs had not yet been unearthed, and they wonder if they are a myth. Who knows what the man was doing when he claimed to be writing his memoirs?

They leave the storage building and return to the house, Beth to do laundry and Esther to cook. Esther confides in Beth she is worried about Manny. He never complains, but Esther can tell he does not feel well. He would not go to a doctor for any reason, and she has no idea what might be wrong. Beth tells her she will pay more attention and see if her dormant nursing skills enable her to make a diagnosis.

Beth has not worked as a nurse for the past five years, feeling burned out. Mostly she is upset about her inability to conceive, and she does not want to be part of the medical community where she is always being reminded of it. Keeping Riley satisfies her need in one way, but it creates a feeling of emptiness and depression in another. She and Gary have discussed adoption as an alternative but have not yet taken steps in that direction.

Beth thinks about her sister-in-law. She, too, is a nurse. They had laughed about the Livingston boys needing so much care they had both married nursing students. Anna is more ambitious than Beth, and she would be working on her master's degree if she had not been kidnapped.

Alan files his automobile insurance claim and starts driving Anna's car, which made it through the fire, until he can decide on a truck. The car smells like smoke, but it still makes him feel closer to her. God is keeping him in his right mind despite his tendency to lose it.

The calm and peace that envelopes him could be from no source other than God. He prays for Jason Stone. A life filled with hate is no life at all, and revenge never yields happiness.

Alan calls Gary. "Hello, big brother. Did you get anything else from the guy in jail?"

"No, he has been quiet. I don't know if he talked to his lawyer yet about his earlier interview."

"Anything on the explosion?"

"No. This kidnapper is one of the best I have seen on safeguarding his identity. Keep the faith, Alan. I know it is hard, but God has a plan in all this. We just can't see it, though Larry's and his old man's salvation are part of it."

As soon as he hung up with Gary, Alan's phone rang. "Hello."

"Hi, Alan, it's Corinne. I called because I may have a little news."

Alan called Gary. "I got some information from Corinne. Charles called someone and discussed ways to bring me down. Corinne couldn't, of course, hear the other end of the conversation."

Gary said, "Maybe we have enough evidence to get a subpoena."

Alan goes to the hospital and prays with the families. One new patient is a little girl who was burned when she tipped a pot of boiling water off the stove. It is so sad to see her and her parents.

After the hospital, Alan goes to one of the nursing homes. He visits several residents, some of whom seem as spry as he is, and others barely able to move. He prays with each one and feels God's presence when he prays. The administrator asks Alan to visit a man he has not seen before, Mr. Partlow. When he goes into the man's room, he sees it is full of photos and newspaper clippings of the Vietnam War. Mr. Partlow sits in a wheelchair at the foot of the bed.

"Sir, are you a veteran of the Vietnam War?"

"My son was. His body was never found."

"Oh my, the pain and suffering you have been through. Let me pray for you."

"Okay."

Alan places his hands on Mr. Partlow's shoulders and prays, "Dear Lord, I come to you on behalf of Mr. Partlow, who has a very heavy heart. He has carried the grief and suffering in his heart for so long, and it is so unbearable; he has great need of your mercy and grace. Please, in the precious name of Jesus, visit Mr. Partlow now and in the days and nights ahead. Be his comforter, his mighty fortress, his place of refuge. Save him, Lord, for your glory. This I pray in the name of Jesus."

When Alan opens his eyes, he sees Mr. Partlow weeping. Alan is crying too. He shares in Mr. Partlow's pain, and he prays that if Mr. Partlow does not know the Lord, he will very soon.

Mr. Partlow looks up at Alan and says, "Your prayer must have made it to heaven, for I have never felt the love and comfort I felt while you were praying."

Alan explains how the love and comfort comes by faith in Jesus Christ. Mr. Partlow prays to receive Jesus as his Savior, and for the first time since he had been told of his son's disappearance, he smiles. He tells Alan he knows his son is in heaven because his son told him of his conversion the last time they talked. He just had not been able to forgive God until Alan prayed for him.

"Anna," said Maria, "I get that God is powerful, but 'knows every hair on my head'? Come on, that's just too much."

"Think of it this way. God created you and knows everything about you. He loves you like a father, though better, and he cares about all the details of your life, including the small stuff. You can ask him to help you with anything, and he will. When I lived at home, I frequently lost things, like my keys, and usually did not find them until after I prayed. He cares."

Larry and Molly return after a short honeymoon in Gulf Shores, Alabama. They stopped there and decided not to continue to Florida. Sunburned and happy, they show up at the Sunset to see Mr. Reed and to check in with their employer. Larry thinks his father looks happier than when they had left and said so. Mr. Reed tells them he is in a Bible study at the home and is growing in his faith. He asks them about their trip.

"It was great!" said Larry. "Just too short."

"We are glad to see you doing so well, Mr. Reed," said Molly.

"Molly," said Mr. Reed, "you need to start calling me Dad."

"Okay, Dad."

Beth and Esther spend the day reading Mrs. Livingston's diary. Much of it is about things only she would have cared about, such as social functions, engagements, and the like. But there was a serious side to the lady. One entry hinted at the idea of a third child in the family, stating, "Bobby has his father's eyes." It seems the child might have died, but he is mentioned again later. "Bobby is not feeling well today, so Esther kept him while I took Gary to the birthday party."

"Esther?"

Esther said, "Bobby was not Mrs. Livingston's biological child, but a child fathered by Mr. Livingston with one of his research assistants. The assistant had given him an ultimatum: if he did not adopt the child, she would have an abortion. He could not abide her aborting the baby, so he told his wife the whole sordid story and brought the baby home. This was just a few weeks before Gary was born. Mrs. Livingston had a difficult time accepting the child, as it reminded her of her husband's infidelity.

"When the boy turned four years old, he disappeared. No one, including Mrs. Livingston, knew what happened to him. The possibilities were numerous: the boy died; the biological mother took him; he was placed in an orphanage. Mrs. Livingston was never quite the same after losing Bobby. She had Gary and Alan and loved them, but she still showed signs of sadness. He was never spoken of again once he was gone.

"Unless Mr. Livingston's memoirs are more revealing, we may never know what happened to Bobby."

"My, what a story," said Beth. "How could Mr. Livingston be unfaithful? Mrs. Livingston looked beautiful in all the photographs. Couldn't you and Manny have found out what happened to Bobby? It's hard to believe nobody other than Mr. Livingston knew."

"We were treated like hired help, which is what we were. No one confided in us, and we were not in any position to know, or ask about, their intimate secrets."

"Why haven't you ever told the boys or me about this?"

"We thought we should not tell since their parents didn't, but I have always thought they deserve to know their family history," said Esther.

"Yes, I agree," said Beth. "They deserve to know. It may not have anything to do with the investigation, but it does have to do with their lives."

Alan gets home a little while before Gary and can tell, from the long faces of Beth and Esther, they had found something important. He resists the urge to question them and asks about Riley instead. They tell him Manny and Honcho took Riley fishing.

Gary arrives, and the group assembles. Esther tells them the sad story of Bobby. The brothers ask many questions, and the answers to most are unknown.

Alan said, "I can't believe our father would do this. Why didn't they tell us we had a brother?"

Gary said, "Who knows? Esther, do you know the last name of Joline?"

"Yes, it's Hall, I think, but she may have committed suicide."

"How about we ask Mac to investigate this and see if he can find Bobby?"

"Mac," said Gary, "how is the work on the associates?"

"I'm about through. Have you got something else for me?"

Gary said, "We just learned that we have a half-brother, and we'd like you to find him."

Mac asked, "What is the boy's name?"

"The only name we know is Bobby or maybe Robert. He was a Livingston but may have undergone a name change. As to his disappearance, he may have died. He was a sickly child according to my mother's diary. He may have been reacquired by his birth mother, Joline Hall; placed in an orphanage; or adopted by a friend or associate of the Livingstons. These are guesses. Finding the truth is your job."

The next morning, Charles is driving to the church. He is almost over the flu, but he does not see the truck behind him until it is too late. The truck runs into the back of his car, pulls back, and does it again and again. Just when he thinks he cannot take any more, the truck pulls around him and drives away.

He is too hurt and upset to think about getting a tag number or a description of the truck. He pulls to the side of the road and checks the back of his car. It is pushed in, lights hanging, window blown out, upholstery torn and flying in the breeze. The car is barely drivable, and Charles can barely drive.

Charles's neck and upper back feel like they are twisted into a knot. When he makes it to his office, he collapses into his chair and begins to shake uncontrollably. He is in this state when Corinne arrives.

"Brother Charles, you look terrible."

For a long while, Charles just sat there shaking. Finally, he said, "My neck and back really hurt, but I am unnerved more than anything. The driver behind me did not ram his truck into my car once. He did it three times, like he was trying to hurt me as much as possible."

"Did you get his tag number?"

"No, I didn't even look."

"Have you called the police?"

"There's nothing they can do without a tag number."

"It can help with your insurance claim."

"Do you mind taking me to the ER?"

"Let me get my keys."

Charles limps painfully to her car. He opens the door and lowers himself into the seat with a muffled scream.

That evening when they convene in the library, Gary said, "There is little doubt the rear-end collision was an attack, not an accident. The insurance company totaled the car, and Charles was admitted to the hospital.

"Investigating this as an attack raises interesting questions. Who attacked Charles? Why did they attack Charles? Is the attack on Charles related to the kidnapping? If so, how? We'll let you know when we get some answers to these questions," said Gary.

Alan asked, "Are Charles Winters and Jason Stone involved in the kidnapping?"

"I am now thinking it is more likely than not. Charles has been reporting to someone, and he wants to bring you down. Maybe his brush with death will cause him to cooperate."

"Oh, by the way," said Gary, "we could not get any phone records on Charles. Nothing. He must have been using a throwaway phone."

"As much trouble as Charles has caused me, I know he just experienced a traumatic and life-threatening experience. He sustained some serious injuries. I will be praying for him." said Alan.

Beth said, "Hello, boys, what's up?"

"You've heard about Charles?" asked Gary.

"Yes, we talked to Corinne," Beth said. "We also finished your mother's diary. She painted a lovely picture of your family with her words. She loved the two of you so much. Bobby is not mentioned again. And that is all we found today. 'I don't know about tomorrow; I just live from day to day,'" sang Beth.

Esther continued, "'I don't borrow from its sunshine, for its skies may turn to gray; I don't worry over the future for I know what Jesus said; and today I'll walk beside him, for he knows what is ahead.'"

Both women sang the chorus: "'Many things about tomorrow, I don't seem to understand; but I know who holds tomorrow, and I know who holds my hand.'"

"I get the impression we'll have to wait until tomorrow," said Gary, smiling. "I hope that doesn't apply to dinner too!"

"Good morning, Gary," says Milton, as he stands at the door of Gary's office.

Gary said, "I hope you haven't been waiting long."

"I've been here long enough to try your coffee. I have some good news. They caught the guy who rear-ended Charles. By some luck or divine intervention, the damaged truck was seen parked in front of a local country restaurant in a small community not far from here where nothing goes unnoticed or unreported.

"A local deputy hears about the incident on his scanner and proceeds to check out the truck. By the time the driver emerges, the deputy has completed his examination and invites the driver to accompany him to the sheriff's office. When he refuses, the good deputy, whose name is Harry Blum, said, 'Well, in that case, you are under arrest.'

"The driver, Jeff Hanson, is in the custody of Sheriff Hellman."

"Has he said anything?"

"Not yet. I imagine he was banged around a bit when he was hammering Charles."

"Esther, look at this," said Beth, as she looks through the stack of papers that are lying by her chair. "It is more information on the Jason Stone matter, written by Mr. Livingston. It says a few people stood firm with the Stone fellow, including a couple with the last name of Winters.

"We will show this list to Gary and Alan and let them figure out what to do. Charles is probably related. It might even be his parents or other close family."

"I don't remember the Winters family very well," said Esther.

Anna knows she and Maria are getting along better since Maria turned her life over to Jesus. It is as though her personality changed overnight. Anna's hormones are wreaking havoc with her emotions, so her personality has changed too. She reclines on the sofa while Maria empties the dishwasher.

"Maria, what's for lunch today?"

"Anna, it's only nine o'clock, and we just had breakfast a couple of hours ago. You are hungry already? I have never been pregnant or around anyone who was, so these things are new to me. I'm glad they're not new to you."

"Yes, I remember the hunger. I'm not supposed to overeat, even though gaining weight is expected."

"Do you think Mary got hungry on the road to Bethlehem?" asked Maria.

"She must have. I cannot imagine having to walk ninety miles while pregnant and delivering my baby in a stable. I read that some theologians dispute the view Jesus was born in a stable, but I am not going to doubt God's Word. What matters is Jesus came to save us."

"I agree, and I will fix you a snack. Just sit right there. I'll even serve."

"Corinne," said Brother Charles, from his hospital bed, "my ex-wife and my two children are in El Paso. I doubt they will come to see me, but I should call them. Also, I have a half-sister in New Orleans; she might care more, but still she probably will not come. Hand me my phone, and I'll get their numbers for you."

"Mrs. Winters, I'm calling for Charles. He is in the hospital."

"Why?"

"He had a car accident."

"How is he?"

"He's hurt pretty bad."

"I can't come, but please tell him I'm sorry. You might want to call Dave Lindsey. He cares a lot about Charles."

"June, I'm calling for your brother, Charles. He had a car accident and is in the hospital."

"Thank you for calling me. Tell Charles I love him, and I'll get my Christian friends to pray for him."

"Alan, have you heard of Dave Lindsey? Brother Charles suggested he preach next Sunday. I'm supposed to ask him when I call to tell him about the accident."

"No, but that doesn't mean anything. Hold up on your call to him."

A few minutes later, Alan reports to Corinne, "This Lindsey fellow preaches mostly on end-times. There are some who question his fixation on this portion of scripture, but I do not find it too unusual. My emphasis is Christian persecution, and I do not think that is strange. Anyway, if he is available, bring him on!"

"Hello, Charles," said Alan. "Dave Lindsey says he will preach in your place on Sunday."

CHAPTER 15

The boss calls Hank to discuss what happened with Jeff. Until then, Hank did not know Jeff had been arrested. The boss says he will be in touch and might have Hank do damage control. Hank thinks it is time for him to escape. Jeff will have to make it on his own. He books his flight.

The next morning, Gary helps question Jeff Hanson. Jeff gives up his partner, Hank Richards.

"Who did Hank take orders from?"

"I don't know the man's name or anything about him."

"Why did you try to kill Charles Winters?"

"I didn't try to kill him. I was told to give him a good scare, and that's what I tried to do."

Jeff is charged with attempted vehicular homicide and auto theft, as the vehicle Jeff drove had been stolen two nights before in Memphis.

Coming away from the questioning, Gary knows Jeff and Hank did more for the boss than attack Charles. He knew from Mr. Benton that they directed the accusers. A few days in the slammer often opened lips, so he would wait a while for further questioning.

―⸺∞⸺―

The Good News Church is slowly regaining its members and adding more after some had been frightened away. Brother Dave Lindsey fills in for Charles Winters.

Alan appreciates Dave, and he tells him so. Dave asks Alan for directions to the hospital to visit Charles, and Alan asks him to lunch with the family before going to the hospital. Dave agrees.

"Everybody, please welcome today's preacher, Brother Dave Lindsey."

The Livingstons make a place for Dave to sit at the large dining table. Dave removes his suit jacket and says the blessing. Then the interrogation begins.

"Dave, where did you grow up?"

"Actually, I grew up near here. Charles and I knew each other as children. We lost touch and then reconnected when he and his girlfriend came to me for pre-marriage counseling. Though I am only a few years older than Charles, he apparently considers me a role model."

"Since you grew up here, do you remember anything about a preacher named Stone who was fired after he attacked Jews and Catholics in the pulpit?"

"Yes, I have a dim memory. My parents wanted to forgive the man and let him stay. They thought they could re-educate him. Others wanted to get rid of him. There was a fight that divided the church, and many people were hurt."

―⸺∞⸺―

After Dave left, everyone met in the library to study the list. Beth said, "Is there a Lindsey on the list?"

"Yes, there is," said Esther. "There are also the Winters who supported the preacher.

Gary said, "Charles may be related to the Stones. That would explain his relationship with Jason."

"Good morning, everyone," said Beth, as she doles out the biscuits. "Since we are finding guys from the past, the kidnapper may show up in our research."

As he slathered molasses on his biscuit, Gary said, "Good."

"Do you want us to get help in order to speed up?"

"No, just keep it between yourselves."

"Oh, no," said Gary to Alan, holding out the *Daily Journal*. "Good News made the front page again. This time, it is the history of the church. It says Reverend Stone preached against Jews and Catholics a few decades ago, and the church never acknowledged its history or made amends to the community."

"The deacons will not be happy about this," said Alan. "But if they make the connection between Reverend Stone and Jason Stone, they'll have a better idea why Jason made such a commotion at our church. Guess I will go to the church and get ready for the onslaught. Are you headed to the station, Gary?"

"Yes. I will see if Jim Boren has a court date. We might be able to talk a plea deal, but I do not think he has much helpful information. He might know more than I think, though, if he's questioned by a skilled investigator."

Alan asked, "Do you know any of those?"

"Ha. You'd better repent for your sarcasm. Remember the Greek meaning of sarcasm is to tear flesh like dogs," said Gary.

Alan said, "There you go showing off again. You'd better repent for being prideful."

"Good morning Corinne," said Alan. "Have you been to see Charles?"

"Yes, he says he is still in pain, but he enjoyed the visit from Dave Lindsey. I told him Brother Lindsey did a good job preaching yesterday.

"He said he knew he would. He asked if there had been any mail he needed to tend to. I told him I would check and visit him again this evening," said Corinne.

"Did you see this morning's newspaper?"

"No."

Alan hands her the paper. "There's an article in here about the church's history. Read it and tell me what you think. I'll be in the office."

After reading the article, Corinne enters his office and says she has never heard anything like that about the church.

"Good morning, this is Alan Livingston. I am calling about the article about our church. I wonder if you can tell me how it came to your attention, why you didn't call the church, that kind of thing."

"Mr. Livingston, I am Sam Levine, editor of the paper. I know your association with the Good News Church, but I also know you are on leave, so that is why I did not contact you. I tried to contact your replacement but was told he is in the hospital, so I decided to run the story and print a response from the church later. Do you want to come over so we can speak in person?"

Alan sits in front of Sam's desk. Sam continues, "As to how the story came to my attention, I've always known it. My parents lived here during that time, and I have been aware of the story since I was a young boy. The hate from the pulpit of the church infiltrated the school. I took abuse from classmates.

"We had a lull in the news, so it occurred to me to revive the old story of the attack on our religion by a former pastor of your church. This opinion was reached in part because the church has already been in the news because of the accusations brought against you. If you wish to respond to the article, be my guest."

"What do you expect the church today to do to make amends?"

"Maybe you need do nothing more than publicly acknowledge it and then address it, hopefully to make sure it doesn't happen again."

"An interesting thing, Mr. Levine, is that my parents were on your parents' side. They were instrumental in getting Reverend Stone fired for his hate-filled speech about the Jews and the Catholics. I assume you are Jewish."

"You assume correctly, and I am glad your parents stood up for us. We are amazed to find Christian pastors who do not support Jews even though Jesus was and is a Jew."

"Are you a Messianic Jew and my brother in the faith?"

Mac said to Gary, "I exhausted my search for the death of the Livingston child, assuming his death would have been in the United States."

"So, this means he is alive?"

"I'm not sure. All I can say is he is not dead if his name is Bobby Livingston. He could have another name if, for example, his name was changed by adoptive parents, which is usual unless it is an open adoption. Maybe we will be able to get his new name from an adoption agency if he was adopted, although some states do not allow that. I wanted you to know where I am.

"Oh, and I have found one guy I want to talk to you and Alan about, a man named Donny Aldridge."

Anna is reading her Bible when Maria interrupts her concentration.

"Anna, there is a doctor who makes house calls for all kinds of issues. The only problem is if you said anything about your situation as a kidnapping victim, my boss might hurt your family, and I will still have to carry my gun."

"I cannot believe you would hold a gun on me, especially since you have accepted Jesus as your Savior."

"I must still work for my employer and do what I am hired to do."

"You know threatening me and working for your employer to instill fear in me do not please God. I will go without seeing a doctor unless I have an emergency.

"My plan to ask you to help me escape is, I suppose, out of the question. All you would have to do is forget to lock my door one night and leave your keys on the counter."

"You don't want to know what would happen to me."

"I do want to know."

"I can't tell you, Anna. As much as I care for you, there is a line I cannot cross."

Mr. Reed is in the hospital following a major stroke. Larry is by his side, holding his limp hand. He has not moved or spoken.

Alan steps inside the door and gives Larry a hug. "How is he, Larry?"

"He's not talking, and I'm not sure if he understands what I'm saying. I'm waiting to talk to the doctor, but I've got to get my work done at the Sunset."

"I can wait for the doctor," said Alan. "Go to work. I'll be here."

It is not long after Larry left when one of the doctors comes in and says, "Mr. Reed has suffered serious damage to his brain, so I'm not sure how much of his faculties he will recover. He is breathing on his own. It's a waiting game."

"What do I tell his son?"

"I don't want to raise his expectations. This may be as good as it gets, that breathing is all we see. He may start talking, but he may not."

Alan calls Larry and passes on the doctor's report.

His time with Mr. Reed would be best spent praying for him, and he turns his attention to the Lord, thanking him for the opportunity. He then focuses his prayer on all the scriptures where the Lord healed someone. He also looks to the Old Testament, where it is promised the "Sun of Righteousness shall arise with healing in his wings," to people who fear the Lord's name. He prays this prayer for Mr. Reed, asking the Lord to heal Mr. Reed so he can feel the Son rising with healing wings over his body and his mind.

By the time Larry returns, the Lord has received almost nonstop communication from Alan about Mr. Reed for four hours.

"Hello, Pastor Alan," said Larry.

Mr. Reed said, "Larry?"

Larry cried out, "Dad! You can talk!"

Alan said, "Praise the Lord!"

―⁂―

Alan leaves the hospital praising the Lord that Mr. Reed is talking despite the odds. *When God is involved*, thought Alan, *odds do not matter!* Once he reaches the compound, he goes to see

Esther in the building where all the boxes of papers were. "Hi, Esther. How's it going?"

"Hi, Alan. We found more papers regarding the Stone matter, and a few papers regarding Bobby. He was an amazing little boy. Your mother came to love him, even though he was from an adulterous affair. He was bright, talkative, curious about everything. I hope Mac can find him.

"As to the Stone matter, your parents tried to find out what happened to Reverend Stone. He seemed to have changed from a normal person to a hateful person who did nothing but preach against the Jews and Catholics. They could never find an incident where Stone was hurt in any way by a Jew or Catholic. They could not find anything to explain why Stone went off the rails."

"Hi, Alan," Beth said. "Jon wants you to call him soon, and Riley needs some friends his age. I know he sees other kids at Sunday School and at Vacation Bible School, but he needs more time with kids his age."

Alan sits down at the kitchen table while Beth continues, "There are some mothers and kids who get together three afternoons a week. Would it be okay for me to take him to these outings?"

"I think it will be fine. What does Honcho say?"

"Honcho says he will be wherever Riley is."

CHAPTER 16

Alan remains standing when he enters Jon's house, until Jon motions for him to take a seat in the living room.

Jon said, "Anna went through a trauma when she was about fifteen that no girl should have to endure. I would rather she tell you herself, but given the circumstances, maybe she will forgive me. Her mother's brother raped her, and we talked her into having an abortion when she found out she was pregnant. We didn't believe Cliff did it."

Alan said, "This explains many things about her and her fears. Oh, God, please heal Anna from all her woundedness and keep her from further harm, I pray in the name of Jesus.

"What is this man's name, and where is he?"

"His name is Cliff Minor, but I don't know where he is. He joined the marines and left soon after getting another girl pregnant."

"We'll find him.

"It's hard to believe you and Linda talked Anna into having an abortion. What were you thinking?"

"Alan, I ask you to forgive me. It was a terrible thing we did. When we learned the truth about Cliff, we banned him from ever returning to our home, and Linda talked her parents into disinheriting him."

Alan has the day by himself since Corinne is off. He calls the worship leader to make sure she and her team are coming to the Wednesday-night service. He calls the head deacon and suggests having a meeting to discuss the immediate future and the newspaper article. He agrees.

He invites Sam Levine to lunch.

"Thanks, Sam, for coming on such short notice."

"That's how everything is in the news. I wouldn't know how to operate except on short notice."

They place their orders, get their drinks, and lean back in their booth, inhaling the smell of barbeque.

"Alan, why did you invite me to lunch?"

"Sam, I took a liking to you and want to know more about you. You know, get acquainted."

"You mean you don't want anything from me?"

"Nothing I can think of."

"I never get invited out to a meal unless the person who invites me wants something. It is refreshing for my lunch partner not to be expecting anything. Thank you."

As they finish their barbeque, the waitress brings them coffee and pecan pie with ice cream for dessert.

"So," Alan said, "did you stay here the whole time, or did you move away and then come back?"

"I left as soon as I got out of high school. Life here was too dull. I went to school in Florida, graduated, and stayed there because I liked the area. Unemployed for a while, I finally landed a job in journalism. I worked there for many years until my parents needed help. My wife and I moved back here to take care of them. The editor of the paper here was ready to retire, and I showed up at the right time to take his place. How about you?"

"I grew up in DC, with frequent visits to Mississippi, and went to college in North Carolina. Along the way, I developed an appetite for alcohol, which became an addiction, which caused me to drop out of college and return home. My parents paid for my rehab. Gary was in the navy at the time.

"I went to an inpatient program in the state capital. While there, I recommitted my life to the Lord. I found a good AA program in Meridian, where I met a Methodist minister and felt God was calling me to be a minister. I went to Memphis for seminary and met Anna there. She was a nursing student."

Alan motions for the check and says, "That's more than you wanted to know, I'm sure. I got carried away. By the way, I have not had any alcohol since rehab, but I have been tempted many times. It is God. There's no other way I could remain sober."

Alan decides to visit Mr. Partlow, who put his faith in Jesus at his last visit. He goes to his room, but all the photos and news clippings had been removed from the walls, and the bed had no sheets on it. He goes to the nurses' station to see if Mr. Partlow had been moved. They said he died in his sleep the night after Alan's visit. His visit with Mr. Partlow was a divine appointment.

In his other visits, Alan's spirit is filled to overflowing with love. After an afternoon of visiting, the compound is a sight he is thankful to see. He and Anna and Riley will probably stay here once she comes home, because theirs is gone and because it already feels like home to Riley and him.

"Alan," said Gary, "Mac found a man named Donny Aldridge."

"I remember Donny. He had a girlfriend named Betty Walton from about the second or third grade to high school. Betty and I started dating during our senior year, and she broke up with Donny. We later split up when we went to different colleges.

"I cannot imagine he would kidnap Anna, but it might seem

like the same thing I did to him. He could be the one. I wonder what Donny did after high school. I figured when Betty and I broke up, she might have gone back to him."

Gary said, "Mac may know; he'll want to talk to you about Donny and others when the two of you can get together."

"Anna's dad, Jon, told me about a man today. We can discuss him in the security office."

"Sounds serious."

"It is. Close the door, please. Anna never told me about this. Please don't tell anyone."

"I won't."

After Alan tells Gary about the rape and abortion, Gary says, "We are here for you, Alan. We will find Cliff. And we will get Anna back."

At the church Wednesday morning, Alan tells Corinne, "Brother Charles is still in the hospital, so I suppose I will have to plan our service for tonight, but I will stay behind the scenes. The worship leader will be here, along with her team. Worship and prayer will be it. If you do not mind, Corinne, call the deacons and tell them we are meeting after the service."

Corinne makes the calls and says, "Brother Alan, Mr. Wesson said he does not take orders from you, and he will not be here. Mr. Brown also said he could not make it. Mr. Whitney said something about the accusations I don't want to repeat."

"Well, call them back and tell them Brother Charles wants them to meet. They have two issues: how to handle Brother Charles's absence and how to respond to the newspaper article."

"The deacons may not like the fact you're taking charge, having been placed on leave."

"That's why I've got the worship leader leading worship and

prayer. My only contribution is to attend the deacon meeting, and I may get kicked out of that!"

"Mr. Marks, thank you for coming down to the station today. I have some questions for your client, Jim Boren."

"Jim is pleading not guilty to kidnapping and arson. He had nothing to do with either, he says. Do you want to question him, Detective? You may, though I imagine he will have nothing to say."

"Joe," said Gary, "bring Jim Boren to the interview room, please."

"Mr. Boren, I'm here to ask a few questions."

"I'm not going to answer any questions, Detective. I plead the fifth."

"I must remind you, Mr. Boren, that you gave testimony previously in this matter to me, having waived your rights. As part of that testimony, you stated, 'This kidnapping was our first,' after admitting you had been involved in a couple of burglaries with Roger Cutlow."

Mr. Marks said, "Detective Livingston, I object. I cannot believe you interviewed my client without my representation. What were you thinking? I will bring this up with the chief and with the court. Plus, I have not even seen a transcript."

"We will provide you with a transcript today. Your client initiated the interview. He wanted to talk. He signed a waiver. You were not representing him at the time. Ask him."

"I'll do that if you'll leave us," said Mr. Marks.

Gary leaves and calls Sheriff Hellman.

"Hello, Detective, this is Deputy Blum. Sheriff Hellman is out of the office. We still have Jeff Hanson in custody. The district attorney is presenting the case to the grand jury next week.

We expect they will charge Hanson with attempted vehicular homicide. We will give you a call."

As planned, Angie Wood leads the Wednesday-night worship and prayer and announces the deacon meeting.

The board meets in the church library. The head of the board stands and addresses the deacons. "Gentlemen, we are gathered here for two reasons. The first is to decide what to do while our interim pastor, Charles Winters, is in the hospital. The second is to decide how to respond to a newspaper article saying our church is guilty of hostility to Jews and Catholics in the past and calling upon our church to make amends.

"We are pleased to have Nathan Horowitz with us tonight, who can answer our legal questions. In fact, maybe Mr. Horowitz will serve as the board's legal counsel. Everyone here knows you and is familiar with your work with the Christian organizations in our community. Do I hear a motion to ask Mr. Horowitz to be our counsel? Okay, and a second? Okay. All in favor? All opposed? Unanimous. Congratulations, and welcome to the board, if you accept."

Nathan nods his head.

"Brother Alan," the head of the board continues, "will you address the two issues?"

"Yes, Charles is in bad shape and may be facing surgery. He needs our prayers, visits, and assistance. I will be glad to help while he is incapacitated, or I will help find someone else.

"As to the newspaper article, some of you may remember the church in the days when Reverend Stone was the preacher. He was, by the way, the father of Jason Stone, who addressed our church not too many Sundays ago. As the newspaper stated, Reverend Stone maligned Jews and Catholics. He was eventually fired.

"In my opinion, and the opinion of Sam Levine, the editor of the paper, this church should acknowledge the sin publicly and address the issue by taking an official stand against such hatred. That is all I have to say, unless you have questions."

"Pastor Alan, thank you for your information and advice. We will ask you to leave us so we can discuss the issue of replacing Brother Charles. If you will wait in your office, we will let you know when we need you to return."

The meeting continues. The head of the board puts the question of a replacement for Charles Winters to the members.

One member said, "Why not just bring Alan back?"

Another deacon said, "Alan needs to stay on leave until his wife is found."

Yet another said, "You mean he needs to stay on leave because he's accused of sexual misconduct and fraud."

They decide to keep Alan on leave and to ask Joshua Strange to take the pulpit in the interim.

As to the newspaper article, the deacons agree for Brother Alan to prepare the response.

Alan says nothing when he is told the results. He will not be the interim preacher for the interim preacher, but he is expected to write the response to the newspaper article. Charles Winters and Jason Stone will be glad he is still cut off from leading his church.

After everyone leaves the church, Alan goes into the sanctuary and sinks down on a pew in the back. The enemy of his soul had managed to take everything away from him except his son and his Lord. He cannot even pray. He remembers the Bible verse in Romans that says the Holy Spirit makes intercession for us when we do not know how to pray. He needs the Holy Spirit more than ever, for he has never lost so much or felt so low.

The next morning, Gary and Alan listen to Beth and Esther tell about their recent finds in the Livingston papers. Mr. Livingston paid Ms. Joline Hall more than $100,000 for not having an abortion and for the costs associated with the pregnancy.

"So, our brother Bobby was an expensive child," said Gary. "The idea of another brother is surreal, and I hope we find him.

"Hi, Mac, we were wondering if you've found anything else about Bobby."

"Hi, guys. I have not gotten far. I have discovered Joline Hall did not commit suicide. She left the research company, and she is living in Tuscaloosa, Alabama. She is married with three children."

"Maria," said Anna, "I am growing and feeling pregnant. We can have our Bible study before lunch."

"Have you forgiven me for my earlier comments?"

"I've forgiven you, but they leave me with a bad feeling, and I don't want to talk about it. I want to study God's Word."

"I'll get my Bible. By the way, I have been memorizing scripture verses like you suggested, and I find myself saying them when I am working or just hanging out.

"The boss said he will send for you the day after tomorrow. Do you want to get something new to wear, your hair cut, nails done? One of boss's men would be on the scene, watching your every move, and yes, I would have my gun."

"I do not want to go shopping or do any of the other things. I do not want to take the chance. I will just wear what I have and fix my own hair and do my own nails. I do not want to impress your boss anyway. Maybe if he does not like me, he will let me go."

Alan visits Charles to tell him the results of the deacon meeting. Charles looks surprised but keeps any comments to himself.

"We know about your family's involvement with Jason's father, Charles, so the charade about not knowing Jason and being surprised is over. I am upset you lied to me and acted like you were my friend."

"I don't know what you are talking about. My family was not involved in any Stone business, and I have not met with Jason Stone. I am your friend, Alan; I can't believe you would think otherwise."

"Well, the facts speak for themselves. I will not bother you anymore. The deacons decided not to reinstate me, and Joshua Strange is your replacement. I'm sure that makes you happy."

"How are you, Mr. Reed?"

"Hello, Pastor. I am much better since I got released from the hospital. How are you holding up?"

"I'm doing the best I can. Are Larry and Molly taking good care of you?"

"Yes, I couldn't ask for a better son and daughter-in-law. They both work here, you know, so I get to see them every day, and they are always doting on me, making me feel loved."

Everyone is planning a surprise party for Gary, complete with birthday hats and a cake with candles, the works. Riley is the most excited, of course, and his excitement is contagious. They turn the lights off in the kitchen and wait. When Gary turns the lights on, everyone jumps out and yells, and Gary gets the surprise of his life.

"Got you!" said Alan. "We finally managed to leave you

open-mouthed and speechless! Ha! Get your birthday hat on, blow out the candles, and we'll hurry up dinner so we can have cake and ice cream."

"You guys surprised me. I almost had a coronary!"

"Uncle Gary, why would you have a canary?"

"Riley, you've got a point. I do not want a canary. But this is a nice surprise, and I thank you!"

CHAPTER 17

Alan tells his family, "The deacons decided not to have me back while Charles is recuperating, and I'm not sure what will happen after that."

"Oh, Alan, we thought you would replace Charles while he is in the hospital, but it's not like you've been fired."

"Yes, it came as a surprise to me. They will ask Joshua Strange to replace Charles. The good news is God is in control. If I hold on … excuse me," said Alan as he flees the kitchen.

No one knows how to comfort Alan, so they leave him alone. This is an unexpected blow, especially coming when his wife is being held by a kidnapper.

On the back porch, Alan is fighting a spiritual battle. There is a part of him not completely surrendered. He wants a drink, a strong drink and more than one. He must win this battle over alcohol, he knows, for his wife and son and himself and, most of all, for the Lord. He cannot let the enemy win. God will bring him through this tribulation. He prays until he overcomes the temptation, at least for the present, looking up at the star-filled sky as he whispers his thanks to God.

After dinner, Alan tells Gary, "I talked to Charles, and he denied everything about his relationship with Jason Stone."

"Well," said Gary, "we didn't really expect him to break down in tears and confess."

Alan said, "I thought he might confess, since he is in the hospital, facing possible surgery. I guess he is too satisfied by the victory over me."

Gary said, "The note found in his papers and the fact that the Winters's name is on the list of Stone supporters highly suggest his family's and his involvement, even without a confession. I now believe we will find his and Jason's activities are connected to the kidnapper.

"We need to find out if the Winters family on the Stone supporter list is the same as Charles's family."

Alan said, "There are two people we can ask, Sam Levine and Jason Stone. Sam would have known Charles, I think, since they both are older. I will call Sam in the morning. If he does not remember, you pay Jason a visit. Maybe you will make a better impression on him than I did.

"Anyway, I'm going to read to Riley and call it a night. Happy Birthday, Gary, and many, many more!"

"Good morning, Mac. I did not expect you to be so early. How about a cup of coffee?"

"Sure, Gary. I have developed a real taste for your police station coffee. It is like no other. I thought maybe we should review our suspects."

"As you know, says Gary, " Jim Boren is in custody. He has been charged by the grand jury of kidnapping and arson. Larry said Boren talked about the kidnapping, and Boren admitted being involved. His attorney, however, says he will contest the admissibility of the admission. The only evidence on the arson charge against Boren is he smelled like smoke when he was picked up.

"The second defendant is Jeff Hanson. He has not been indicted but will be next week for attempted vehicular homicide. Hanson was found with the truck that rammed into Charles Allen's car.

"Then we have several suspects not yet arrested: Roger Cutlow, Hank Edwards, Charles Winters, Jason Stone, Donny Aldridge and Cliff Minor—quite a group!

"Of course, it might not be any of them, but I think it probably is. We need you to keep looking at these and any others you unearth, and to continue your search for our brother. Do you have a statement for me?"

"Anna, your meeting with the boss is tomorrow."

"I can't think of anything else. I don't understand what he wants from me." Anna looks around at the small, neat house and knows she should have appreciated what she had. She is about to step into the unknown.

"I have enjoyed our time together, Maria, and I pray you will continue to grow strong in the Lord. I will continue to pray for you even after we have parted ways."

"Oh, Anna, don't forget me, and I will not forget you. By introducing me to Jesus, you changed my life forever."

"I am glad. I do not want to meet the boss. I just want to return to my husband and child."

Gary thinks about the suspect for the kidnapping and arson. He wants to see the results of Mac's investigations.

"As to Donny Aldridge," Mac said, "you know about the early years, so I focused on Donny's life after high school. I interviewed a teacher, who was best friends with Donny's mother, who also taught at the local community college. Donny spent a lot of time there during his childhood and beyond. The teacher, Mrs. Fair, met me in the cafeteria."

"Mrs. Fair, do you know if Donny dated other girls besides Betty?"

"Yes, he dated several girls, but he did not get serious about any of them."

"What did he do after high school?"

"He went to college in New York and majored in accounting."

"When was your last contact with him?"

"After he finished college, he came back to see me, and he unloaded about Alan and Betty. He had strong feelings against them both but especially against Alan for stealing Betty from him.

"Oh, I did see him one more time, after his parents died. He was still angry at Alan, saying he would have married Betty if 'the Livingston pervert had stayed out of the way.' I remember his exact language because he was so forceful. He also said he would 'make Alan pay someday.'"

Gary believes Donny makes the best suspect from the facts they know so far. He is not local, so he can get things done without getting caught. He has had many years to nurse his grudge and work out his plan to torment Alan. Their next steps are to question him and to investigate any relationship between him and the other suspects.

Alan usually spends his days at the church preparing sermons, meeting with people, and taking care of church business. As things stand now, he goes to the church and gathers some of his personal items. Corinne is there. She is upset Alan is still on leave.

He tells her he has been upset too, but he reminds himself that God is in control.

Alan goes by the newspaper office and asks Sam about the Winters family. Sam said, "I think the Winters family in Reverend Stone's day is Charles's family. I can find out for sure by checking the historical record. Why do you ask?"

"We think Charles is involved in the kidnapping."

Alan prays while he drives to the compound. In addition to giving thanks and praying for Anna, he prays for a long list of people. He also prays for the persecuted around the world and for the country of Israel. He arrives at the compound with no memory of driving.

Everyone is tired, so all retire to their quarters early. Alan reads to Riley and prays with him and waits until he goes to sleep. Gary is eating dessert when Alan comes into the kitchen and sits on a stool.

Gary said, "How did your talk with Sam go?"

Alan said, "He is checking through the history and will get back to me. Also, I went by to see Charles again today. He is better and going to physical therapy rather than having surgery."

"Have you found out anything more about Donny?"

Gary said, "Mac interviewed a teacher who knows him. He still hates you."

"I'm not surprised. What about the other suspects identified by Mac?"

"The only ones he has investigated besides Jason Stone are Donny Aldridge and Cliff Minor. Mac is also searching for our brother. We captured Cutlow near the police department. He may have a contact inside the force."

Alan said, "The inside source could be that Eddie Baker guy who thinks I kidnapped my wife and burned down our house."

Anna wakes up praying. She dreads meeting the boss and prays for God's protection and for him to use her to reach this man for God's purposes. Maria is making coffee and says, "Maybe the boss just wants to meet you, and you'll come back."

"Maybe. I cannot eat anything. I think I would throw up. I'm so nervous."

"Remember, Anna, God will be with you. He will never leave or forsake you."

"Oh, Maria, it warms my heart to hear you say that. You are the sunshine in this otherwise gloomy day."

Maria answers the phone. She looks at Anna and says, "The boss is ready to see you. His assistant is coming after you. He will be here soon."

"Hello, Mrs. Livingston," he says as he puts the blindfold on her and leads her away.

Alan kneels at the altar to worship and pray. He is so blessed to feel he is wrapped in God's love. He believes all the promises of God and feels certain Anna will be returned to him, and the church business will be done in accordance with the Lord's will. He lies on his face in total submission to the creator of the universe.

Still feeling the full effects of having been in God's presence, Alan walks to the kitchen, where he runs into Corinne, who is making chicory coffee to go with her homemade beignets. Alan feels like he has been transported to New Orleans.

"So, how are you this morning, Pastor?"

"God is on the throne. How are you?"

"I'm enjoying life, Pastor. God is good! My husband got a raise. My daughter's summer job is going great. The only downside is my son does not like summer camp, but I am praying and believing God will change either the camp or my son's heart or both."

Alan goes into his office and opens his Bible to renew his mind. He finds the promise in Jeremiah 29:11, where God promises to give us "a future and a hope" and to listen to us when we pray. This verse meant so much to Alan during his rehabilitation and AA meetings, and it means even more in his current situation. In 1 Corinthians 18, Paul says the cross is the "power of God" to those who are being saved. Alan prays and meditates on the Word until he is fortified and ready to leave.

Gary gets the criminal history information on Donny Aldridge. He finds that Donny had been convicted of cheating on his income tax returns and misappropriating client funds, for which he lost his CPA license and spent some time in prison. Gary also finds from another source that Donny has substantial wealth from writing an accounting textbook and appearing at accounting conferences.

"Good morning, Milton. I am calling about a suspect identified for us by Mac. His name is Donny Aldridge.

"His beef is with Alan and goes back to high school days. We know he could have done the crimes; he had motive and opportunity and resources. His hatred for Alan is serious. What we need is someone who knows him, perhaps worked with him at his old accounting firm. We need to move fast on this guy."

"I'll get right on it, Gary. It is not that unusual for a perpetrator's motive to date back to high school days. Tell Mac he hasn't lost his touch."

CHAPTER 18

"Mrs. Livingston, I will now lead you into the office of the boss. You will keep your blindfold on unless he tells you to take it off. You will sit here. Would like you something to drink?"

"Yes, I will keep the blindfold on. No, I do not want anything to drink."

Anna feels a presence in the room that unnerves her after the assistant leaves. She wishes she could disappear.

"Mrs. Livingston, I am, for lack of a better description, the boss. How are you today?"

The voice sounds like a robot. She says, "I am nervous and being blindfolded makes me more nervous."

"I apologize, but it is necessary. Is Maria taking good care of you?"

"Yes, Maria and I have become friends."

"Maria is a good woman. I understand you are pregnant. I also know about your Christian witness to her, which does not surprise me. I am sure you wonder why you were kidnapped, why you are here. The answer is simple. Your husband needs to be taught a lesson."

She is blown away by his intimate knowledge and directness. She has never felt so violated except that one time when she was a teenager.

"Your pregnancy is a potential problem. I don't suppose you would consider abortion?"

Anna responds sincerely with a trembling voice, "I would die before I would have an abortion."

"I guess that answers that question. Any reason you are so against abortion?"

"One reason is that I consider abortion to be the murder of a human being created by God. Another reason is I had an abortion when I was fifteen. I have never completely recovered. I know I will see my baby in heaven, but I pray often when feelings of guilt and shame overtake me, even though I know God has forgiven me. I would rather die than commit murder."

Anna leans back in her seat and asks for a drink of water. The memory of her abortion is almost more than she can bear in the home of her kidnapper and in the early stages of pregnancy away from her husband.

"I appreciate someone who has strong convictions. Should I decide abortion is necessary, your convictions will not stop me, but I am not inclined to order you to abort."

She cried out, "Why would you?"

"Because you are carrying Alan's child," he said.

"Maria, thank God I got to come back," she says as she slumps onto the sofa. "He was so frightening! I have never been that scared! He knows everything we have ever said to each other. He said he might make me have an abortion. You did not know this about me, but it would kill me to have another abortion. I simply would not survive. We must pray."

Maria hands Anna a glass of juice and said, "But you survived. God was with you."

"Yes, the boss says he will send for me again. I do not think I can go. Why does he want to see me again?"

"Anna, I don't understand the boss and what motivates his actions. He does not tell me anything, so whatever I say is a guess. We should count our blessings."

Gary meets with the accountant who exonerated Alan, and he is again angered his brother was falsely accused. At least now there is proof.

As he enters the security office, Gary asks, "How is everything, Honcho?"

"All good. Riley is getting a kick out of being with the other kids in the afternoon outings. He holds his own with the older boys without getting mad or crying. He's a big boy in a little-boy body."

"Yeah, he has grown up a lot, and I'm glad he's experiencing childhood. Some kids miss it altogether when something like this happens."

"Quite true," said Honcho. "How's the search for Bobby going?"

"Mac concluded he's not dead if he is using the name of Bobby or Robert Livingston. I believe Mac is now canvassing adoption agencies to see if he went through their systems. That process usually requires court orders to gain access. Mac is good at that, having been trained as a lawyer before joining the FBI. Still, it's a time-consuming process."

"Alan looks happy."

"Yeah, he got some good news today. I'll let him tell you."

Alan said, "Hey, you guys, what's going on?"

"I need to ask you the same thing," said Honcho.

Alan tells Honcho the news until Beth calls everyone in for dinner. Gary then announces there is absolute proof Alan did not embezzle any money from the church-building fund or any other fund in the universe.

As everyone is sleeping except the guards, a man moves along the perimeter of the property, setting up explosive devices against the outside of the fence in several locations. Then he sets them all off, waking everyone but Riley.

One of the guards reports the explosions caused minor damage to the stone fence. The guards believe they were set off mainly to harass and torment the residents rather than to breach compound security.

Everyone returns to their rooms to go back to bed and worry. Alan tries to turn his worry into prayer as he considers worry sinful and useless in changing anything. He can recite the scriptures where God says not to worry. So, he tries and tries again.

"Good morning, Jon. I thought you might be up early. How are you?"

"Better than I've been for a long time, Alan. I have a new lady in my life. Lisa Love was Linda's home health care nurse. After Linda died, Lisa and I stayed in touch. A few weeks ago, Lisa stopped by to check on me. One thing led to another, and now we are seeing each other every weekend."

"Great. I'm happy for you, and Anna will be too."

"You're out early today. Any reason in particular?"

"Normally I would be going in to finish my sermon for tomorrow, but I'm still on leave. I am just going in to get my thoughts together before the day really heats up. Maybe Joshua Strange, the new replacement for Charles, will be there."

When he arrives at the church, his phone rings. "Hello, Alan," said Charles. "They are about to discharge me, and I wondered if you could give me a ride to my house."

"Sure, Charles. Just call me when you have been discharged, and I'll head your way."

Alan's phone rings again, caller unknown.

"Is this Alan Livingston?"

"Yes. Who's this?"

"I am your worst nightmare. I took your wife. You will not get your wife back unless you carefully follow my instructions. You will get them soon."

The man hangs up. Alan quickly writes the words down so he can give them to Gary. Of course, there is not much Gary can do with just a bunch of words. About that time, Charles calls to let him know he is ready to leave.

Alan takes Charles to get his medicine and groceries. He tries to connect with Alan, saying, "I know you're mad at me, but I can't be anyone but me, and if that's not good enough for you—"

"Charles," Alan said, "you are not shooting straight with me, but there's nothing I can do about it, and I don't want to talk about it."

Alan finds Gary in the library and tells him about the call.

"Did you recognize his voice?"

"No, I was paying attention to what he was saying, and, as usual, he was using something to change his voice."

"Well, at least you have the words written down. We will get the phone records, but I am sure he used a throwaway phone. I wonder what he will require for Anna to be released back to you."

"I don't know, Gary. All I know is I will do anything, so long as it does not hurt anyone, to get Anna home."

The presence of God during praise and worship remained through the sermon. Joshua Strange was an anointed preacher, and two people came to the altar to receive Jesus as their Lord and Savior. Alan knew God was working in their hearts long before they came forward. The celebration in heaven over these two is awesome. If, as some believe, loved ones can glimpse those still on earth, the family and friends of the ones just saved are rejoicing with the angels.

It is a good Sunday even if Alan did not get to preach. He enjoys hearing Joshua, and he tells him so. Alan is thankful he has been delivered from alcohol and called to preach, and he knows God is not through with him yet.

Beth and Esther regale Alan and Gary with the details of their ancestry. Riley says, "Aunt Beth, did you know my daddy and my uncle Gary when they were little like me?"

"I didn't," said Aunt Beth, "but Aunt Esther did. She helped take care of them when their parents were busy, like she and I help take care of you."

"Uncle Manny and Mr. Honcho do too."

"Yes, we do," said Honcho, "and we are very honored to be part of your life. You are a mighty fine young man."

Beth said, "Today is one of Riley's playdate days."

"Good," said Alan. "I'm glad you set that up for him."

"Nathan, it's Alan Livingston. Do you have any spare time today?"

"Yes, Alan. How about lunch?"

"That would be great." Alan thinks of the new Thai restaurant.

"Barry," said Alan, "how's the insurance business this morning?"

"It's good, Alan. How are you?"

"I'm okay, but I'll be better when I get my check."

"You haven't gotten it yet?"

"Nope."

"Call me back in about thirty minutes."

Alan called Maxine at the bank while he was giving Barry his thirty minutes. Maxine told Alan in no uncertain terms he would have to make his payment on time or incur a penalty.

"Okay, Barry, your thirty minutes is up. Don't tell me—the check is in the mail."

"Ha! The check *is* in the mail. In fact, it was mailed last Wednesday, so it should be there by tomorrow at the latest."

After they place their orders, Nathan said, "You picked a great place, Alan."

Alan said, "Thanks. I think so too. Nathan, I want you to know there is proof I did not embezzle church funds."

Nathan said, "That is no surprise to me, Alan. I'm glad there is proof."

"But we can't tell anyone about the proof yet, so don't say anything to anyone."

"I won't. How are you otherwise, Alan?"

"I am surviving."

Alan also tells Nathan about his disappointment of not being allowed to fill in for Charles. Nathan says he is sure it would work out.

At Memphis the next day, while sitting in Milton's office, Gary asks Bo Wilson, "How do you know Donny Aldridge?"

"We worked together at the accounting firm."

"What kind of coworker was Donny?"

"He was meticulous, and he got very emotional whenever he found mistakes, including his own."

"Is that unusual?"

"Yes, at least with him," Bo said. "He went way over the line, berating people and using obscenities."

"I'm surprised he didn't get fired. Did you associate with him outside the firm?"

"He did get fired, and I think he had some legal troubles, maybe even went to prison. We were not really friends, but we did and still do have a meal together every now and then at the country club where we are both members."

"Does Donny ever talk about Alan and Anna?"

"Alan is an obsession for Donny. He cannot get over Alan taking his girl away from him in high school. He only mentions Anna when he says he doesn't see how she could be married to such a terrible guy."

"Has he ever done anything besides talk about Alan?"

"Yes, he hires people to watch Alan, especially around the holidays."

"What does he do with the information?"

"I don't know, but he is definitely unhinged mentally."

Milton asks a few questions, and they ask Bo if he would invite Donny to the country club for dinner and try to get him to talk about Alan. He agrees, saying, "Maybe he'll slip and tell me something other than his usual vitriol."

"Okay, Bo, we appreciate your help, and we'll be in touch. Let us know when you set up a date, and we'll have you stop by here and get wired."

After Bo leaves, Gary turns to Milton and says, "What do you think about that? Aldridge is a real nutcase, isn't he?"

"Yes, he may be our man."

CHAPTER 19

"Alan, this is your nightmare again. Your wife has a surprise for you. I do not want to spoil it. I haven't decided yet whether she will keep it or lose it."

Alan tries to put down the exact words of the kidnapper. He does not know what to think. Why would the kidnapper decide whether Anna would keep or lose the surprise?"

Beth answers on the first ring, saying, "Hi, Alan, how are you?"

"Well, not too good, because I just got a call from the kidnapper. He told me Anna has a surprise for me if she does not lose the surprise. He also told me he can make her lose the surprise. What do you think he's talking about?"

"I don't know," Beth said, thinking she does know but not for sure, and she does not want to tell Alan over the phone. She said, "Why don't you come on home, and we can discuss it?"

"I tried to call Gary but got his voicemail. Do you know where he is?"

"He's probably on his way back from Memphis. He went to question someone who knows Donny Aldridge. He should be home soon."

"I'll see you in a few minutes."

"Alan," said Gary, "what did he say this time?"

"Oh, it was so strange, Gary. He said Anna has a surprise for me if she doesn't lose it and if he doesn't make her lose it."

"That is strange. What kind of surprise could Anna have for you?"

"I can't think of anything. The only thing would be if she, if she, no, she could not be, uh, pregnant. You think she could be? If that is it, then he is saying he could make her have an abortion. Oh, Lord God, please protect Anna, and if she is with child, please protect the child. What do you think, Beth?"

"I think you're right. It is the only thing that makes sense the way he said it."

"Gary, do you agree?"

"Yes."

Alan sits on the couch and says, "I want to be excited, but I am devastated by his threat. Why would he do that?"

"To harm you in yet another way, but he did not say he is going to make her lose it."

"We must pray like we've never prayed before." Alan wept.

"Dad, I got another call from the kidnapper, and from what he said, it seems that Anna may be pregnant."

"Oh, no!"

Alan gives Jon a pat on the shoulder. And, as they sit down, he says, "It is our child, I think, Dad."

"Are you sure it isn't the kidnapper's child?"

"I don't think so. Anna hasn't been gone that long, and the kidnapper would have boasted if it were his child."

"It feels like she has been gone a long time."

"It does, doesn't it? I believe she will come home, but it will be in God's time, not ours. Goodbye, Dad. God will see us through."

Gary calls Milton to see if Bo has been able to set dinner up with Donny. Milton said he has, and Bo is coming by the office later.

A short time after Gary arrives, Bo is wired and goes to the club.

Gary asks Milton, "Will an agent be nearby in case Bo is caught?"

"Yes," said Milton, "one of our agents is a member of the club, mainly to play golf, but occasionally it works to our advantage. He will have dinner with his wife, so he will not stand out. Patience, my good man."

Gary has trouble sitting still while waiting. He said, "We've not caught any breaks in this case. It has been about two months, and we have three suspects in jail, but none is the kidnapper, and none seems to know the kidnapper."

When Bo returns, everyone is surprised to hear Donny say, "Nothing is bad enough for that slimeball preacher." He also says that Alan "will really cry when something happens to his young son."

"He clearly hates Alan," said Milton, "and I would watch that boy around the clock."

"No kidding," said Gary, "but did he kidnap Anna and burn their home?"

Gary sits at a table in the security office where he will not be bothered. He reviews what Mac has written about Jason Stone. Most of the information is from old newspapers and interviews with some old-timers.

"Jason's grandfather lost the family farm to a bank run by a Jewish banker. He was arrested for trying to kill the banker. After his arrest, he was visited by the sheriff's brother-in-law, a Catholic priest from Memphis. The priest and Jason's grandfather almost had a fight.

"The grandfather's wife and two oldest sons were arrested also for related crimes, and the younger children, including Jason's dad, were placed in homes. Charles's grandparents took in Jason's dad.

"The grandfather became a preacher in prison, but he never let go of his hatred for the banker, sheriff, and priest. His son, Jason's dad, also became a preacher. When he preached against Jews and Catholics, your parents helped get him fired.

"Jason's motive for his message to the church is revenge for his dad. Sam Levine found it was Charles Winters's grandparents who parented Jason's father, so Charles must have known Jason's dad and Jason, so Charles also has grounds for revenge. Whether either of them kidnapped Anna or burned their house is questionable. I do not think Jason is sophisticated enough, and Charles's motive may not be strong enough. They most likely have been working for the kidnapper."

Alan and Gary meet in the choir room at the church to discuss the suspects and their associates. Gary said, "The suspects in custody are Roger Cutlow, Jim Boren, and Jeff Hanson. While these three participated in the kidnapping, house fire, and related activities, we do not believe any of them planned the kidnapping or know who did.

"Our kidnapper may be Donny Aldridge. Donny has conflicts with the dates of the kidnapping and the arson, but it is unlikely the kidnapper is personally involved.

"Milton just found one of the private investigators hired by Donny. We are interviewing him tomorrow."

Alan said, "It has been a long time since the kidnapping. You would think with the FBI, police department, and private investigator all working, more progress would have been made."

"It's almost time for supper. I will see you back at the compound. Oh, by the way, how's Charles Winters?"

Alan said, "He seems okay, and he should be back at the church soon. We'll see what the deacons come up with, which reminds me, I have finally written a response to the newspaper article about the history of the church and need to get the deacons' approval before getting it over to Sam. Would you mind reading it?"

"Maria, are you going to join me? I am starving. I can't go to sleep if I'm starving."

"You can't be starving. We just ate a huge meal an hour or so ago. You don't want to gain too much weight."

"The book you got me that I'm reading now says I can gain twenty-five to thirty-five pounds since I'm at a healthy weight."

"Yes, but that's over a nine-month period. At the rate you are going, you will gain forty to fifty pounds!"

"You are being a mother hen. If we have milkshakes, I can sleep, and my baby will be well fed."

"You win. If you are making them, I will take strawberry. Tomorrow is your day to spend time with the boss. Are you nervous?"

"Yes, but God has got this. I am going to rest tonight and get ready in the morning. I'm not going to let the boss take away my night."

Brother Joshua calls to ask Alan to hold the Wednesday-night service in his place. Alan jumps up from his chair in the library and shouts, "Hallelujah." He looks at the verse in Philippians about pressing on toward what Jesus has called us to be and do, and the verse in Hebrews about running with endurance our race toward Jesus.

These verses make up his working-out teaching, which includes the verse about how we are to "work out our own salvation through fear and trembling," in Philippians. It seems like he is working his out that way, and he is having a hard time staying in the race. It is God who keeps him from tearing into someone; it is God who keeps him sober; and it is God who will work everything out.

Sitting in front of Gary's desk, which is covered in papers, Mac said, "This situation revolves around the suicide of a young man.

"His name was Emory Walker, and his parents are Edward and Olga Walker. Emory consulted Alan when he was home from college to talk about whether he could be a Christian and a homosexual. He did not tell his parents he was a homosexual and did not have plans to do so."

Mac goes to get coffee and continues when he returns to Gary's office. Mac misses being in law enforcement and soaks up the sweaty and smoky smells of the small-town station.

"It is probable that Alan counseled the young man that homosexuality is a sin and showed him the scriptures to back up the statement. He must have told him Jesus forgives us of our sins if we repent and ask for his forgiveness and that Jesus could deliver him from his homosexual desires. They had several sessions according to Emory's roommate.

"After Emory returned to college, the Walkers moved away."

Mac continued, "About a year later, Emory committed suicide, leaving a note stating he could not resolve the conflict between being a homosexual and being a Christian. The note said being a

Christian was more important, and he would rather lose his life than lose his salvation."

Gary drops his head and shakes it upon hearing about Emory's suicide and his reasons for taking his life. Beth had a cousin whose daughter committed suicide, and the family was never a family again, so great was the pain and loss.

"The Walkers did not notify Alan of their son's suicide. Instead, they told everyone Alan was responsible. That is how I found out about it. I was asking around about Bobby and used the Livingston name. A man told me a preacher named Livingston caused a young man to commit suicide. I questioned him, and he said the parents talked about getting even with Alan for their son's death.

"So, Gary, Alan doesn't know about this. I do not have any more information, but I am still working on it. This is going to hit Alan hard."

"Yes, Mac, you're right. I will pray about the best time to tell him. If he calls you, tell him to talk to me."

The boss says, "Hello, Mrs. Livingston. I propose we discuss your future. Does that agree with you?"

"Yes, I can only hope you plan to release me," said Anna, as she noticed for the first time that the house had a super clean smell of furniture polish and carpet cleaner but seemed large and empty.

The boss said, "That is a possibility, hence the blindfold. Your husband may have suffered enough, but sometimes I think he takes the easy way out."

"What do you mean?"

"His faith seems to keep him going, like it's magic or something."

"It's not magic, but it is supernatural, for God is supernatural.

He is real, and he answers our prayers even though it is not always what we want. He gives us peace."

"A year ago, I would have thought you crazy, but after hearing you and Maria during the time since I kidnapped you, I think maybe there is something to this God of yours."

"I will be happy to tell you what I know so you can make a decision about whether to follow him."

"Thank you for sharing with me. I have listened to all your conversations with Maria, and I have heard sermons by your husband. I must say I get as much from your conversations as I do from his sermons. Do you think your God would forgive me for kidnapping you and for all my other sins, as you call them?"

"Yes, absolutely God will forgive you if you repent of your sins and ask him to be your Lord and Savior. He will not only forgive you of your sins but also remove them from you as far as the east is from the west."

Gary and Alan are in the compound library when Gary said, "I hate to tell you this."

"Gary, I'm having a bad year, to say the least, and I am not easily shocked. Just tell me."

Gary hesitates but then said succinctly, "Emory Walker committed suicide, and his parents blame you."

Alan raises his hands to heaven and cries out, "Oh, God, have mercy on me! I should not have lost touch with the young man. I cannot believe it. It is my fault. I should have insisted on staying in touch and continued my counseling. I do not even know if he followed up online. Somehow, I doubt it. I just cannot believe it. How could I have messed up so badly and done such a horrible thing?"

He falls to his knees and prays, "Oh, God, please forgive me for this terrible sin. I know I do not deserve your forgiveness, but I ask for it anyway. Please bless the Walker family and give them the comfort and peace only you can give. Lead me, Lord, in whatever I should do for this family."

Looking up at Gary, Alan said, "Gary, I feel so worn down and unable to cope with this tragedy. I cannot even imagine how horrible the Walkers must feel about losing their son. I am thankful he knew Jesus as his Lord and Savior, but that is no relief unless they too are saved.

"Maybe I will have the opportunity to meet the Walkers and ask for their forgiveness. Until then, I will pray for them. My prayer is for God's will to be done in their lives as well as ours. I also pray for the kidnapper and his cohorts to know Jesus as their Lord and Savior. God is a miracle-working God. We should never underestimate him and his goodness."

Anna is excited when she tells Maria, "You won't believe the most incredible thing—the boss asked me about God and said he would think about what I told him!"

"Anna, you can't possibly be telling me this. You cannot possibly be serious. Now tell me what really happened."

"Maria, you are right. It is not possible, but we serve a God of the impossible. Did he not create the world with his word? Can he not move mountains? Did Jesus not die on the cross and rise again that the world might be saved?"

"Oh, Anna."

"What do you think will happen next?"

"I guess, Anna, we will wait just like we've been doing."

"At least there is one thing we know for sure: God is in control."

Gary checks on the status of the suspects. Hanson pled guilty to aggravated assault, a felony, which carries a penalty ranging from five to sixty years, and arson, which has a penalty of five to twenty years, with damages. The arson charge was possible because of testimony by Jim Boren. Hanson received a fifteen-year sentence and a $5,000 fine.

Gary prevailed on the admissibility of Boren's testimony, and Boren pled guilty to first-degree arson and kidnapping. Kidnapping in Mississippi carries a life sentence by a jury or one to thirty years by a judge. Boren received a ten-year sentence. His sentence was light because of his testimony against Hanson and Cutlow.

Cutlow's case is not disposed of because the judge had not ruled on the motion to dismiss. Given Boren's testimony, a favorable ruling looked unlikely.

Gary calls Alan because he knows Alan will want to visit the men in prison, both to discuss their information and to witness to them about Jesus.

Gary and Milton interview Donny's private investigator, John Nelson, at Milton's office. "Mr. Nelson," said Gary, "what can you tell us about Donny?"

"He had me stake out the church to spy on Alan. One of my buddies staked out the home. He knew Alan's every move."

Milton asked, "What's his name?"

"Louis Justice."

"What did you see Alan doing at the church that you reported to Donny?"

"He worked irregular hours and spent a lot of time with his secretary. She was there even on her days off. I wouldn't be surprised if he drank and cheated on his wife."

"What did you actually see him doing?"

"He and his secretary hugged when they arrived at the same

time. Other women went into the office and came out looking happier than when they went in, like maybe they had a drink or two while they were in there."

"Did you report this to Donny?"

"Yes, this and a lot more. He was fixated on Alan."

The questioning continues, with Milton and Gary concluding most of the findings by Nelson are conjecture. Yet they agree the reports would have fed Donny's hatred toward Alan and provide justification for his hatred, and the question of how the kidnapper knew Alan was gone is answered.

Mac enters the trailer park and easily finds the one he is looking for. Pretty flowers grew along the sidewalk. He said, "Ms. Joline, it's good of you to see me. I have questions about Bobby."

"How is Bobby?"

"That is what I am trying to find out, along with where he is. Have you spoken with him recently?"

"Heavens no. I lost contact with Bobby when I gave him to Mr. Livingston."

"When you found out you were pregnant, how did you know it was Livingston's child?"

Joline rolls her eyes and plays with a lighter on the table. She said, "He was the only one I had been having an affair with, but the affair was over before I found out I was pregnant."

"Why did you not want to keep the child?"

"I was young. Mr. Livingston was married and not likely to divorce his wife and marry me. I could make money by threatening to have an abortion, which I wanted to have anyway."

Mac looks at the family pictures on the mantel. It is hard to imagine this mother planning to abort a child. He said, "Why did you think you could make money?"

"Mr. Livingston was religious and would never allow his offspring to be aborted, a procedure he equated with murder."

"So, you threatened to have an abortion unless he took the child. Is that correct?"

"Yes, and he had to pay for all my expenses while I was pregnant and for two years after, which I figured was long enough for me to get back in shape."

Joline places the lighter on the coffee table, folds her hands, and gives her full attention to Mac.

"Did you ever threaten to expose or report him to someone?"

"No."

"Why not?"

"I was a willing partner, and I was loyal. He had been my boss for seven years, and I did not want to ruin him. I just wanted him to keep the baby and pay me money."

"When was the last time you saw the child?"

"I gave him up six weeks after he was born, and I saw him a couple of times when I worked with Mr. Livingston at the compound."

"At six weeks, Mr. and Mrs. Livingston took your child. Had you named him?"

"I hadn't named him, and they named him Robert."

"Did he ever get in touch with you after he was older?"

"No, I'm not sure the Livingstons told Bobby about me."

"And you have no idea what happened to him after you gave him up?"

"No. You must understand. I did not want the kid. I would have been fine with aborting him. I certainly did not want to keep up with him or hear from him."

"Do you still feel that way?"

"I've softened a little, having children of my own now. I do not look back unless I am feeling blue. I do not want to see him. He would be a painful reminder of my mistake."

A KIDNAPPING REVIVAL

After a few more questions, Mac said, "God forgives all our mistakes if we repent. I will pray for you."

"I hope you find Bobby. If you do, please tell him I'm sorry."

Alan rings the doorbell and waits at the front door for several minutes. Charles lets him in and, with his walker, moves slowly and stiffly to a chair in the living room. He motions for Alan to have a seat. Alan removes a pile of dirty clothes from the chair and said, "Charles, Joshua Strange is doing a good job filling in for you while I'm on leave. When do you think you'll be able to return?"

"I'm not able to do much of anything right now. I hope I will get stronger with rehab. Have you talked with the bishop?"

"Yes, I called him yesterday. He is concerned about you and said he will talk with you today or tomorrow," said Alan.

"Did you ever get over the idea that I am involved with Jason Stone?"

"No, as a matter of fact, I know your parents supported Jason's father, and my parents did not," said Alan.

"So what?"

"Well, it's just a little too convenient for you to show up when Jason attacks the church where I am the pastor, and to lie about what I said at the conference, implying I had something to do with kidnapping my wife. You also said I gave Jason the go-ahead to disrupt my church. You act like my best friend while you tell lies behind my back," said Alan.

"Alan, I don't know where you are hearing such nonsense, because I have always been on your side. Did I not let you ease out of the conference? Did I not call you and offer my services? Why do you not trust me?"

Alan stands up and says, "You talk out of both sides of your mouth, Charles. Who besides Jason Stone are you working with?

You got rear-ended because you messed up. I'm on to you, Charles, and it won't be long before the police are too."

"Alan, you have no proof. The accident was just an accident."

Alan said, "How about the note saying the 'next job' would be at the compound?"

"I don't know anything about such a note. You are imagining things," said Charles.

Alan whirled around and left.

Alan said to Riley, "Hello there, partner. How about you and I go find Manny?"

"He's at the barn," said Riley.

"Let's go see him."

"There he is," said Riley, as he runs over to get a hug from Manny. Manny grins from ear to ear to see Riley, and they talk together for a while. It is apparent to Alan that Riley and Manny are great friends. He is glad but a little jealous.

Gary places the chess board on the table in the library and lays out the pieces. They start the game, and Alan said, "Gary, I talked to Charles today. Guess what he wants me to believe.

"He said he has no interest in and does not know Jason Stone. He said he played it straight with me the whole time.

"Charles is as crooked as they come. I do not know if he did anything more. This whole thing makes me a little confused and crazy."

They play while talking, and Gary said, "I can see Charles being involved in the kidnapping but not as the main player, and the same goes for Jason Stone. Jason is out for revenge and would not have said no to money. Charles would want revenge and prestige and would be susceptible to money too. I think they worked together. Checkmate."

"Hey, that's not fair. You know I can't multitask!"

Gary laughed and said, "Jason got to exact revenge on a descendant of someone who voted against his father. Charles was probably promised your church. What do you think?"

"He wants me to lose the church. He wants to take it away from me. Charles and Jason want me gone permanently, but you and I know God is not through with us yet.

"The kidnapping was intended to inflict injury on me, and the kidnapper has not hurt Anna, though being ripped from your family and home is hurtful. God will work a miracle in keeping the church alive, and he will work a miracle in keeping Anna in good health, and our marriage too. I believe this with my whole heart."

Alan returns to prayer and studying the Bible. Not preaching is no reason to stop studying God's Word. He realizes how close he had come to losing his church entirely. Before he could get going, Riley comes in to ask him to read him a story. He feels so blessed to have Riley and immediately goes to search for just the right story. He chooses the story of Jonah, which he knows has a lot more going for it than a big fish.

Once Riley falls asleep, Alan joins Gary in the kitchen, grabs a Coke, and says, "What about Roger?"

Gary said, "I get the impression Roger is higher in the organization than Jim Boren or Jeff Hanson. Unfortunately, the evidence is weak against him, but that is to be expected for someone at a higher level. If there is one thing we know about this kidnapper, he is a pro at protecting his identity. Roger may walk."

Alan said, "That hardly seems fair. Jim Boren's testimony should be given some weight since he received a substantial sentence. I hope Mac turns up something more soon. We have got to find that kidnapper.

"One other thought I had after visiting Charles. I think I should go back to question Jason Stone, and you should go with me."

"That is a good idea, Alan. We can plan on tomorrow. Maybe we'll have a slow day in law enforcement."

CHAPTER 20

When they arrive at the auto-repair shop, they see Jason. He is stacking tires. Alan said, "Jason, we would like a few minutes of your time."

"What in tarnation do you two want? I don't have any time for you, preacher man," Jason said as he continues his job.

Gary said, "Well, you may not want to talk with my brother, but I am a police detective, and I can take you down to the station. So, we can talk here or at the police station."

"Okay, I'll give you ten minutes. If you do not treat me right, I'm calling a lawyer."

Jason finishes stacking the tires and picks up a large wrench. Gary says, "How long have you known Charles Winters?"

"I don't know him," Jason said, hitting the palm of his hand with the wrench.

"Are you sure about that? Didn't Charles's parents support your parents when it was being determined whether your dad would continue to pastor the church."

"I don't know him."

"That's not what he said."

"Why that lying no-good-for-nothing!"

"So, you do know him. Put the wrench down."

"I told you I don't know him. I don't know what you are talking about."

"I think it was like this. You were paid to take your revenge against Alan by scaring his church members away. You were trying to destroy the church, and Charles Winters was to take the church over. He too wanted revenge, and he was paid as well. Now what we need to know is who paid you and Charles."

"I didn't attack the church. I just told the people the truth about persecution."

Alan said, "Yes, but you spoke on persecution in a way to scare the people so they would renounce their faith or, at least not acknowledge it. That is what you meant to do, scare the people away, so the church, under my leadership, would be destroyed."

"Your ten minutes is up. Please leave."

Gary said, "I don't have to leave now, but I do need to go back to the office to decide what charges to bring against you."

After Jason walks away and Gary and Alan return to the car, Alan said, "What do you think?"

Gary said, "I think Charles is the leader of the two and dealt with the kidnapper. I bet Jason's first move is to call Charles."

Alan said, "I hope nothing bad happens to Jason like it did to Charles."

"Yes, me too. At this point, the boss may think them dispensable, but as far as we know, he has not killed anyone. I'm headed to the station to write up a report on this, and then I'll go see Charles."

"Do you want me to go with you?"

"No, I'll take a patrolman. That might be enough pressure to get Charles to come clean."

"Okay, then I'm off."

—⁂—

"Dad, how are you?"

Jon returns to the sofa and takes the woman's hand in his. They are having tea. Alan's eyes get big.

"Hi, Alan. I am fine. You've met Lisa, haven't you?"

"No, I don't think so. How are you today, ma'am?"

Alan remained standing.

"I'm good," Lisa said as she stands. "If you two would like some privacy, I have some shopping to do."

"No, that's fine. Dad, we are making progress in finding the kidnapper. God is faithful, and I have every reason to believe Anna will be coming home soon."

"Thank you for coming. It means more than you know."

Alan hugged Jon and said, "Take care. God bless you both."

"Hello, Mr. Reed. How are you today?"

"Hello, Alan. I'd like for you to meet Alice Warner." Mr. Reed was sitting on his bed, and she was sitting in a chair by the bed.

"Glad to meet you, Ms. Warner."

"We came here close to the same time, but we've only met recently and have started getting to know each other. We have a lot in common, and we are enjoying each other's company. At least I am."

"I am too. Now, Hubert, you are just looking for a compliment, aren't you, dear?"

"I didn't know your name was Hubert, Mr. Reed. I've never known a Hubert."

Mr. Reed laughed and said, "Are you making fun of my name?"

"Of course not. I like it, but I have to go. Give my best to Larry and Molly. Nice to meet you, Ms. Warner."

Alan enters Mr. Benton's room at the Country Meadows. The woman in the bed looks fragile.

"This is my wife, Eloise. She has been in here for several years. That is why she does not come to church with me. I read the Bible to her, and the home has church services she sometimes attends. How are you?"

Alan sits down in the chair beside Mr. Benton and says, "I'm okay. Progress is slow, and I can hardly wait to see my wife. I believe God will bring her home in his time. My job is to keep praying."

"I pray for her and you and your son too, Pastor Alan. I'm still so sorry for the pain I caused you," said Mr. Benton as he stared at the floor.

"Don't give it another thought, Mr. Benton. I know why you did it, and I think anyone would have done the same thing in your shoes. I know I would have. I'm just thankful nothing bad happened as a result, and you believed in me enough to confide in me," said Alan as he reached over to offer his thanks with a shoulder hug. "I am grateful to God and to you. Has your family from Florida been up for a visit yet?"

"No, they will be here at Christmas. They will want to meet you."

"I want to meet them too. Do you know anyone else here who might need a visit from me?"

"Yes, as a matter of fact, there is a young man three doors down on the right. I don't think he ever gets any visitors."

"Okay, I'll go see him. It was nice to meet you, Mrs. Benton, and good to see you, Mr. Benton. Call me if you need me."

"Hi. My name is Alan Livingston, and I am the pastor of the Good News Methodist Church, where Mr. Benton attends," Alan said as he stood in the doorway.

"My name is Randy Oliver. Come in."

A KIDNAPPING REVIVAL

Alan goes in and sits in a visitor's chair.

Randy says, "I am here because I have had two strokes; the second one paralyzed me. I was placed here by my stepmother after my father died. She could not care for me without his help."

"I am sorry to hear about your strokes. I pray God will heal you. Do you want me to pray with you now?"

"I don't think prayer will do any good."

"Well, it can't hurt now, can it?"

"I guess not, since you put it that way."

Alan reached for Randy's hands and said, "Okay, let's bow our heads and pray."

He began, "Father God, we come to you now in the name of Jesus. I ask you to wrap your loving arms around Randy and give him your comfort and your peace. I pray you will surround him with your love and your healing power. Lord, I pray for healing for Randy, to heal his paralysis and other infirmities, to bring glory to your name, in the mighty name of Jesus. Amen.

"Randy, have you been born again?"

"What do you mean?"

"I mean, have you repented of your sins and asked Jesus to be your Lord and Savior?"

"I did when I was young, but I don't remember much about it."

"Would you like to know more about it?"

"Yes, but not today. Can you come back sometime? I am too tired to continue our conversation now."

"I will definitely come back, and I will be praying for you. Do you have a Bible? Here is a list of scriptures you might want to read. God bless you, Randy."

As Alan ventures toward his office door at the church, he spots another note. He takes the note by its corner and reads its contents.

The note said, "I will provide instructions soon. Your wife is unharmed."

Alan calls Gary, but it goes to his voice mail, and Alan remembers Gary is probably visiting with Charles Winters. He copies the note and saves the original to give to Gary.

As Alan ponders the note, he realizes he is jealous that another man is spending time with his wife. He wonders if it is sinful to be jealous in this instance or if it is just sorrow. He checks his Bible for answers.

One instance of jealousy Alan remembers is in the book of Luke dealing with the prodigal son. The lesson usually focuses on the prodigal son, but the older son was jealous and felt his father treated him unfairly by welcoming the prodigal son home with open arms.

Alan looked at other cases involving perceived unfairness. One was in the book of Jonah, where Jonah was so upset God forgave his country's enemy, he asked God to take his life.

And in Matthew, laborers, who were hired at different times of the day, all agreed to accept the same pay. When those who worked longer did not get more than those who did not work as long, they thought it was unfair.

Corinne clears her throat. Alan looks up from his Bible study and said, "You startled me."

She does not respond and turns to walk away.

Alan said, "You seem a little distant today. Is anything wrong?"

"Not exactly. I had a visitor earlier today, Charles Winters, and he was looking for you," said Corinne.

"When did he come by?"

"Early this morning."

Alan said, "Did he say why he was looking for me?"

"Yes, he said he needs to clear some things up with you right away," said Corinne.

"Did he say anything else?"

"Yes, he said you accused him of kidnapping your wife.

And quite honestly, Pastor Alan, I am having trouble believing you think so badly of Brother Charles, with all he has done to help you."

"I'm sorry, Corinne, but we have evidence Brother Charles worked with Jason Stone in his attack."

"My apologies, Pastor Alan, but I would have to see the evidence before I can believe it. I have always trusted you, but Pastor Charles cares for the church, and he treats me right. He did a good job with Vacation Bible school, and you barely knew what was going on."

"Corinne, you know what a burden I am under with my wife missing. It is not a mystery I barely know what is going on. That's why the church placed me on leave."

"That is not true, Brother Alan. The church placed you on leave because Mary Jo accused you of sexual assault, and Mr. Benton accused you of embezzlement."

"You're right, Corinne, but the church said that I will remain on leave until my wife is found."

"You don't have to lie about it. Why are you harassing me?"

"I'm not harassing you!"

"Yes, you are, and I'm about to call someone if you don't leave now."

"Corinne, what has gotten into you? Has the kidnapper gotten to you? Has he threatened you or someone you love? What is wrong?"

"You are what's wrong, Pastor Alan; no one has gotten to me but you. And now I am calling Charles to tell him you will not leave me alone," said Corinne as she started dialing her phone.

"Charles," Corinne said, "Pastor Alan is harassing me. Will you come to my rescue? Or better, will you call one of the deacons?" Corinne walked away, continuing the conversation.

Alan throws his hands up and shakes his head. He imagines Charles pumping his fists. He closes his door and calls his brother. He has been played by Charles.

"Gary, did you talk with Charles yet?"

"No, he wasn't home when I called on him."

"Apparently he was here at the church this morning. Corinne laid into me on Charles's behalf. Can you come by the church?"

"Yes, I'm not far away."

Alan hides in his office until Gary arrives.

Gary said, "Hi, Corinne," but she does not respond. He walks into Alan's office and asks, "What's wrong with her?"

Alan closes the door and said, "I think she's either working for Charles, or the kidnapper has threatened her with something. She is taking up for Charles and dismissing me."

Gary says, "Well, remember the Bible says not to worry, so don't. You know God has got this, and this, too, shall pass. Do I get the award for the most clichés?

"I got your voicemail about the note."

Alan says, "Yes, the good news is the note confirms Anna is okay.

"As to the clichés, sometimes they help when I'm about to get into worry mode, which has happened a time or two."

"More like a hundred times," said Gary.

"Not that much, but if I listen to my own preaching, worry is fear, and perfect love casts out fear, so where does that leave me? Sorry. I'm talking in circles, but you are right; I am not to worry," said Alan.

Just then Corinne knocks on the door and said Charles wants Alan to call him.

Alan said, "I'll do better than call. My brother and I will go visit him. You can tell him we are on the way."

Alan and Gary leave to go to see Charles. They do not say anything else to Corinne, and she does not say anything to them. They decide to run by the station and get a copy of Mac's report on Jason Stone. They pick it up, and Alan looks it over.

"Do you think a patrolman ought to go instead of me?"

"Yes, probably, but he is expecting you."

"You're right. Let me read the report. You will have to do most of the questioning. Corinne wore me out."

"Okay, here we are. Ready?"

CHAPTER 21

"Hello, Charles. You know my brother, Gary, the police detective. He came along to ask you a few questions. But first, what did you call me about?"

Alan and Gary stand inside the door while Charles slowly makes it back to his chair. He tells them to sit.

"I called you because Corinne called me. I was calling to tell you to knock it off. Your gripe is with me, not her."

"You're right about that last part, but she made it personal. I didn't."

Alan and Gary look around the room. Alan notices the dirty laundry and dishes piled up. Gary notices Charles's pistol on the end table.

"Okay," said Gary, "you guys can work out your differences later. I have some questions, and I want answers. When did you first meet Jason Stone?"

"I have told Alan several times I have not met Jason Stone," said Charles.

"We know you are lying because Jason indicates the two of you have been working together. Also, you had a note in your office with Jason's phone number on it. You need to stop lying and come clean," said Gary.

"You can't believe Jason. He's not very bright," said Charles.

"So, you do know him."

"Not like you think. I have just seen him around. I don't really know him."

Gary rolls his eyes, clears his throat, and said, "In fact, you enlisted Jason's help, or someone told you to enlist Jason's help, to take the church away from Alan. The only reason the plan hasn't succeeded is that you got injured when Hanson hit you from behind, and more importantly, God protected the church and Alan."

"Let's leave God out of this," said Charles.

"God is in control of everything, Charles," said Alan.

"That he is, but let's not pick sides for him."

"Okay, you two, back to the questions. Charles, who is paying you to take the church away from Alan?"

"No one is paying me for anything. I am not trying to take the church away from Alan. I was appointed to serve in his place while he is on leave. There is no giant conspiracy against Alan."

"Charles," said Alan, "my parents were perceived as enemies to Jason Stone's parents and to your parents. That is why the two of you are involved in this scheme to get me. Someone else, who is paying you, wants to get me for other reasons, but the main thrust is to punish me by taking away my wife, my home, and my church."

"Once we get information from you, Charles," said Gary, "you will be out of the picture unless there is evidence you started the fire or helped to kidnap Anna or engaged in other illegal activities at or beyond the church."

Charles asked, "Are you saying something at the church has been illegal other than Alan's sexual assault and embezzlement?"

"If it occurred as part of the kidnapping, it would be," said Gary.

"I don't have anything else to say to you two. Alan, stay away from Corinne. It's not fair of you to harass her," said Charles.

"You are not the only one we want," said Gary. "We also want whoever is paying you. Alan's wife has been gone for over two months. It's time for all of this to stop."

Alan got right in Charles's face and said, "For the love of God, Charles, help us find the man who has Anna. The police do not want you. They want the kidnapper and the arsonist. We think the man who injured you is working for the same man you are. He went overboard on your punishment for leaving that note lying around. He was supposed to scare you, not almost kill you. Haven't you been through enough to see the error of your ways in this, Charles?"

Charles said, "I've asked you to go. If you have more questions, Detective, leave your brother at home."

Gary and Alan leave Charles and proceed to the compound. Alan goes straight to his room and flops on the bed, so Gary entertains Riley.

Not much time passed until Alan emerges to find Gary and Riley playing chess in the library.

"He's good, maybe better than his dad. He beat me twice!"

"Great going there, Riley," said Alan. "I'm hungry. Are the women in the kitchen?"

"I think so," said Gary. "Something smells good, and I think they are about ready to set the table. Riley, go see how they are coming along."

"Gary, back to the kidnapper's note. What did you think?"

"It's great news Anna is fine!"

"I know, Gary, but the weird thing is I'm jealous he's with my wife."

"Jealousy of him is probably easier to handle than fear for her."

"I guess so, but she's still not home."

"I'll take the note in with me tomorrow. Maybe he has made, or will make, a mistake. Here's Honcho. Come take a look at this latest note from the kidnapper."

"Alan, what do you think about it?"

"I don't have a clue, Honcho."

"At least you got a good report on Anna and no more threats."

"My faith is still strong, but I don't know how much longer I can wait."

"Esther and I found an interesting letter today," said Beth, "received by Mr. Livingston from his boss, Ben Abel, who asks several questions about Bobby. The letter was written when he was about three."

"Gary was close to the same age, and Alan was not yet born at this time. We do not know what to make of the letter, if anything. It seems the boss was too interested in Bobby, but maybe he just cared about his employee's family. We'll continue our review tomorrow and let you know if we find anything else."

When Alan arrives at the church, he notices two cars. The sight transports him back to the parking garage in Memphis. Only this time he is at church.

As he passes the sanctuary on his way to his office, he sees Mary Jo Holt kneeling at the altar. Alan prays whether to minister to her or let God work without his intervention. Mary Jo turns around.

"Pastor Alan, I've been wanting to talk to you and apologize for lying about you."

"I understand, Mary Jo, you were under great duress when you made the accusation, and that was why you made it."

"I also held my husband's actions against you, but I confessed my sin to God, and I know he forgave me. I want you to forgive me too."

"You have been forgiven by me for some time now, and I am thankful for this conversation. Your danger is passed, I understand from talking to Mr. Benton, who also recanted his accusation. He was under the same type of duress as you. Don't worry, I won't tell anyone except my brother, and I thank you from the bottom of my heart."

"Thank you for forgiving me."

"I noticed another car out front. Is someone with you?"

A voice was heard from the back of the sanctuary. As the man came into view, he had a 9mm pistol pointed at them.

"No, I'm not with her, but I will be talking about her to the boss, who will be upset, Mary Jo, that you've recanted your story. And, preacher, thanks for letting me know about Mr. Benton. The boss will be upset with him too."

"You are in the house of God," said Alan. "You must confess and repent before it is too late. Turn from your sins now, and you will be amazed at the peace God will give you."

The man said, "Save it, preacher, for someone who cares. I am not the one who decides what to do. I am just a messenger. I tell the truth. What's wrong about that?"

"You know what's wrong with that. I ask you again, do not do this thing. If you confess your sins to God and ask for his forgiveness, Jesus will set you free," said Alan.

"I'm going to confess what I know to my boss. I do not know what he will decide. I am leaving now, and if you know what is good for you, you will not call your brother until I have time to leave the county, at least thirty minutes. I have a partner nearby, and if you don't follow my instructions, I will be back."

The man leaves, and Alan and Mary Jo stand together with their mouths agape. Mary Jo slumps to the floor, crying about her sister, whose life is threatened again. As Mary Jo gets up, Alan realizes Mr. Benton's grandchild is also in danger because of him.

Alan prays for all who had been threatened and for the ones who were doing the threatening. He asks God to change their hearts and disrupt their evil plans.

Mary Jo is shaking all over. Alan wants to reach out to her, but he is reluctant to do so after the accusation. She calls her friend to come get her. Her weeping eases, and she is ready to go home.

After Mary Jo leaves with her friend, Alan calls Gary. It had been at least thirty minutes. Gary answers, and Alan breathes a sigh of relief.

"What's going on?" asks Gary, and Alan tells him about the encounter. Gary said the man making the threats would be arrested if found.

Alan tells Mr. Benton what happened at the church. Mr. Benton's head drops to his chest, and he weeps quietly and says, "I don't want my wife to hear about the new threat. She takes things like this hard, and it will upset her too much."

"I'm so sorry, Mr. Benton. I did not know the man was there, but that does not change what happened. Do you want to pray?"

Driving away, Alan sees the man who appeared in the sanctuary and delivered the threats. Looking at the man, he realizes there is someone else in the vehicle. They were quickly moving away, but he thinks the passenger is Charles. He tries to get their license plate number but fails.

Alan drives to where Charles lives to see if he is there. His car is there, but no one answers the door.

Once at the compound, Alan fills Gary in.

Gary said, "It's certainly possible the man didn't leave and instead drove over to pick up Charles, or Charles is the partner the man spoke about."

"Maybe I didn't see them."

"What does the man look like?"

"He's average height and weight, with brown hair cut short and gray eyes. He has bushy eyebrows, and his nose tilts to the left."

"That's a lot of detail. You must have checked him out when he was threatening Mary Jo."

"Yes, when someone is pointing a pistol at me, I pay close attention."

"We'll keep an eye out for him. What kind of car were they in?"

"An old gray Toyota Camry."

"Okay, we have a little to go on."

"Oh, Maria, some days I am so depressed; if it weren't for my family and my Lord, I might give up; and sometimes I think about doing it anyway. I know Alan and Riley will be so excited about a new member of our family; you are encouraging; and I've received some hope from the boss."

After Anna prays and they have a large dinner, Maria said, "Anna, I've been thinking about what might happen to me. If the boss lets you go, where would he go? Where would I go? I guess my only hope is to go with him."

"I can tell he cares about you, Maria. He said you are a good woman. I do not think he will forget you. You know I have forgiven you, and I have even forgiven those men who took me from my home. That took a lot of prayer and even more time listening to God and reading his Word. As to the boss, I am still praying God will change his heart and he will become a born-again believer. It is hard for me to hate him and pray for him at the same time, so I guess I have forgiven him too."

"You're a good Christian, Anna. If I had not met you, I might have never heard about Jesus, much less made him my Lord. And if the boss gets saved, that will be a miracle, for I know him, and he is a hard man."

"God will forgive him if he truly repents and asks him to be his Lord and Savior. It will not matter that he is a hard man. Good night, Maria. God bless you."

"Good night, Anna, and don't let the red bugs bite!"

"Ha, that's bedbugs, not red bugs, and may they not bite you either!"

The next morning is Sunday, and Alan is at the church early, eager to experience God's presence. He kneels at the altar and prays for the service, for the people, for Anna and many other needs, including Mary Jo and Mr. Benton. Soon the people begin to arrive, and Angie and her team begin playing music.

Joshua preaches on the prodigal son parable. The congregation does not move during the sermon, with all eyes on Josh. As the closing hymn is sung, several come forward to leave feelings of jealousy and other negative emotions at the altar. Others come to pray for their "prodigals."

Alan marvels at how the Holy Spirit works, often giving different people the same message. Alan stands with Joshua at the door and speaks to all the people as they leave. Most shake his hand and speak, though some silently glare at him or look away.

Mr. Benton steps up and said, "Pastor Alan, I've decided to let God handle this whole thing. I cannot protect my grandchild. Only God can. My job is to pray. God already knows the outcome, and I trust him."

"Good for you, Mr. Benton. You are right. God has this, and he has your grandchild in the palm of his hand. I'm glad you came today."

Alan and Joshua finish, and Alan invites him to the compound for dinner with the family. He declines but thanks Alan and tells him he is blessed to be working with him.

The rest of Alan's Sunday is spent with Riley and the folks. They have an early-evening picnic and play games. They play horseshoes, run races, toss balls, and are entertained by the growing puppies. He prays while he watches Riley and the puppies.

CHAPTER 22

Jason Stone runs across his momma's picture album Sunday afternoon, which takes his mind back several years to when they were still at the church. As he looks at the pictures, he remembers how proud he had been of his daddy, and his momma had been too.

One thing different about then and now, Jason realizes, is Jesus had given him peace and joy back then, which he no longer feels. He wonders if it is possible to get that joy back and decides it is not.

Jason reviews his current relationship with Charles and the kidnapping. He never intended to commit a crime, but his need for revenge led him to the life he is living. He needs to get out of it. He does not want to go to prison. He does not want to start over somewhere else; he feels at home in the town of his childhood.

As Jason lies in his bed that night, he thinks about his momma and how much she loved God even after they had been run off from the church. In fact, his daddy also kept his faith in God. He is the only one who left the Lord. He wonders if the Lord would take him back.

Charles Winters is with Arthur Loden in the Toyota Camry

when they call the boss and are instructed to do no more unless they hear from him. The two men are at loose ends. Arthur decides he will get a job with Jason Stone.

Charles is thankful there is no more criminal work available, as he hopes to escape any kind of legal entanglement. He intends to continue with church work. At one time in his life, his church mattered to him, though he never had the passion he saw in others. He certainly never meant to do criminal work.

Gary decides to keep a closer eye on Charles, and he enlists a friend's support, assuring him he is helping rescue Alan's wife. He also checks in with Mac, who reports his wife is hospitalized and he has been spending most of his days at the hospital.

"Is there anything we can do to help you?"

"No, just pray for her recovery and my sanity. You know she has Alzheimer's disease and cannot understand what is being done to her. I try to keep her calm and cooperative, as does our daughter. I have not quit working on your cases; I just have not been able to get out in the field like I need to. The doctors say she will likely be released by the end of the week, so I can get back to it then. I'll let you know."

"We will be praying for you and your wife and other family. I have friends whose parents have dementia, and I know it's a hard path."

Gary and Milton interview Donny at Milton's office. Gary asks, "Donny, when is the last time you saw Alan?"

Squirming in his seat and sweating profusely, Donny said, "I haven't seen him in person since last year. I have seen him on videos since then."

"Are these videos your private investigators made?"

"Some of them are. I also watch the videos of his sermons."

"Where did you see him in person?"

"I saw him and Anna at the Elvis Presley festival, but they didn't see me."

Milton said, "Is that when you got the idea to kidnap Anna?"

"I did not kidnap Anna. I have kept tabs on Alan, and I like it when bad stuff happens to him, but I have not done anything to hurt him. I am not the one you want."

"Your investigators keep a close eye on Alan. That's how you knew he would be out of town."

"I did know, but I did not do anything as a result. I've known all his actions for several years now, but I have not laid a finger on him or his wife or child."

Gary said, "How did you meet Roger Cutlow?"

"I met Roger in prison."

"When did you last speak to Roger?"

"I haven't seen him since he got released before me. I don't know where he is."

"How do you know Arthur Loden?"

"Same answer, but I did see him once since then at a diner."

"Both of these men are involved in the kidnapping, and you want us to believe that you aren't?"

"I'm not."

"When were you in Mantachie?"

"Not in the past few months."

"What if I told you someone saw you there three weeks ago?"

"It's possible. I do go through there from time to time."

"But you said you had not been there for several months."

"Well, I didn't count driving through."

"We need to see your phone, your computer, and your bank account."

"Not without a subpoena, you don't."

"If you have nothing to hide, why not?"

"I have my rights. I'll be getting an attorney."

"Don't go anywhere, Mr. Aldridge. We will want to talk to you again soon, and we'll have that subpoena for you in a couple of days."

After Donny left, Milton said, "Let's lock him up."

Gary said, "Not so fast. We do not have anything on him to tie him to the crime. Roger has not implicated him."

Milton said, "We need to interview Roger. Donny must be guilty. He's so against Alan."

"We need evidence. We will keep digging. You talk to Roger, and I'll see if I can find Arthur Loden."

Milton asked, "Why don't we get Donny to take a polygraph test?"

"That's a good idea. If he is innocent, he will go for it to prove his innocence, and if he's guilty, he'll take it to make us think he's innocent and because he thinks he can beat it."

Gary asked, "Alan, has anything happened?"

Alan said, "There have been no new sightings, no guys with pistols, and no threatening notes."

"Glad to hear it, little brother. Mac's wife is in the hospital, and he has not had much time to attend to our cases. He asked for prayer."

"Well, of course. What is the room number? I'll go by and visit."

Maria said, "The boss wants to see you as soon as you can get ready tomorrow morning."

"Oh, Maria, why so early?"

"Like I know."

Anna is blindfolded and led out the door. When she arrives,

the boss appears almost immediately. She is shaking while she waits to see what he wants.

"Good morning," said the boss. "Thank you for coming on such short notice and so early."

"I didn't have much choice, but you're welcome."

"The reason I have to see you is to ask you some questions. When did you become a Christian?"

Anna takes a deep breath and whispers a quick thank you to God. He answered her prayers. Would the boss take the plunge under the blood of Jesus?

She tells the boss about her Christianity. He says nothing.

———

Gary checks with the neighbor he enlisted to watch Charles. The neighbor says he saw Charles get out of a gray Toyota. When Gary asks him about the driver, he said about the same thing Alan had said.

Gary calls Alan and says, "Alan, you were right about Charles being the passenger in that man's car."

"Guess I'm not losing it after all."

———

Charles calls the bishop and tells him he is healthy enough to take on a church in a regular capacity.

"Brother Winters, aren't you returning to the Good News Church?"

"I'm not sure. Joshua Strange has been covering for me, and as you know, I was covering for Alan, so I do not know where I stand."

"The deacons have not consulted our office. I will get with them on this. I'll let you know what we decide."

"I can't hang out to dry too long. I have bills to pay."

"I understand. If you are not needed at Good News, we'll try to find you a position elsewhere."

Alan visits Mac and his wife at the hospital. Then he goes to the compound for lunch with Esther and Manny. Beth and Honcho are at the skating rink with Riley. He feels at peace and filled with love, dining with the two people who cared for him from the time he was born.

After lunch, Alan runs errands and drives by where their house once stood. Anna had been gone way too long. She just had to be home soon. He prays.

When Alan reaches the church, there is an old decrepit truck sitting at the entrance. Standing nearby is Jason Stone.

"Hello, Jason. Come in."

"Hello, Brother Livingston. I do not think I can come in after so many years. It might make me sad."

"Okay. Do you want to talk out here?"

"No, that's okay. I'll come in."

"Here's the office. What's on your mind?"

"Since you and your brother showed up at the auto-repair shop, I've been thinking," said Jason, looking at the floor, silent for a time.

He finally looks at Alan and, halting after each pronouncement, said, "I want to start over. I do not want to hate any more. I am not happy. I want Jesus to come back to me."

"Jason, Jesus did not leave you. You left him, and if you want to return to him, you must repent of your sins. Ask him to forgive you and restore the relationship you once had with him as your Lord."

"I need to talk to your brother too, but I don't want to go to the police station."

"I can call him to see what he says. Do you want me to do that?"

"Yeah."

"Gary, can you come to the church now to interview Jason Stone?"

"I really need him to come down to the station. You can come with him."

"Jason, he says that you need to go down to the station. I can go with you if you like. Do you want to pray now?"

"Yeah, I need to pray."

"Good. Follow me to the sanctuary."

After praying, they talked about the meeting with Gary.

"I don't want to go down there, Brother Livingston."

"If you want to come clean and not go back to your old life, going to the police station to talk to Gary is a good start. He will see you are treated fairly."

Jason hesitated and then said, "I reckon you're right. I'll go."

"Before you go, can you answer one question for me? Do you know Charles Winters? Did you ever do anything with him?"

"Yeah, I know him. He helped me get ready to come to this church that morning I told your people about persecution."

"Okay. I will call Gary and tell him you are coming over. You are making a good decision, Jason. God bless you in your new walk. You are invited to come to church here. You would be welcome. Most of the folks have forgotten or forgiven you for the persecution speech, and if they haven't, that's their problem."

When Jason gets to the station, Gary is waiting in the interview room. He stands up and reads Jason his rights. Once Jason responds, Gary says, "Jason, why did you appear at the Good News Methodist Church?"

Jason hesitates, then shrugs his shoulders and says, "I wanted to take the church away from Brother Livingston because your parents took the church away from my daddy."

"Did Charles help you with this?"

"Yeah, he coached me."

"What else did you do with Charles?"

"I worked with him and Arthur Loden. Charles and I attacked Ricky Rivers. I knocked him out, and we stole his uniform. There was a cell phone too, in his pocket. I have it."

"Do you have it with you?"

"Yeah, here it is."

"Why did you steal the uniform?"

"Because we were going to kidnap Brother Livingston's son."

Gary's mouth fell open, and his eyes got wide when he heard this, one of their greatest fears.

"What happened?"

"Charles had a wreck and got hurt bad, so we couldn't do it."

"What did you do after Charles got hurt?"

"I kept working at the shop, and I had to get a job for Charles's boss, Arthur Loden."

"What was the connection between the attack against the church and the attack on the security guard?"

"Both were meant to hurt Brother Livingston, the same reason as for the kidnapping."

"Did you have anything to do with the kidnapping?"

"No, sir, but Charles and Arthur talk about it and the boss all the time."

"Is there anything else you can tell us?"

"I'm sorry, and please, I can't go to prison."

"Well, Jason, you know we will charge you with assault today. We will release you with the understanding you will report to us anything you hear from Arthur Loden or Charles Winters. Is that clear?"

"Yes, sir, I can do that."

"By cooperating, you should receive a lighter sentence, perhaps probation, as this is, I assume, your first offense. I will make sure the prosecutor knows you came in voluntarily to give us your statement and confession."

Across town, Mac returns home with his wife and considers the Livingston matters once he gets her settled.

He turns his attention to his search for Bobby. Joline calls him with the name of the lawyer for Dr. Livingston's boss. The name of the boss was Ben Abel, and the name of the lawyer is Art Katz.

Anna punches the cushion as she says, "Maria, can we go somewhere? I have been here for more than two months, and I have not been outside except for going to meet the boss with a blindfold on. I have serious cabin fever."

"Anna, I can't help you. The instructions I have are to keep you inside. The boss may like me, but I do not dare break his rules. He is too powerful, and I am too weak."

"Maria, you are a child of the King of kings. Have you ever heard the children's song 'Jesus Loves Me'? Anyway, it says, 'I am weak, but he is strong.' And the Bible says it many times. God is our strength and our fortress. So, you may be weak, but God is powerful on your behalf."

"Yes, I know, but the boss has authority over me in this situation. At least he is interested in Jesus, and he may change if we keep praying. How does that song go?"

"I'll sing it for you, but we need to eat lunch first. My singing may spoil your appetite."

Sitting in the retired lawyer's opulent dwelling, Mac begins his interview of Art Katz, saying, "Thank you for seeing me. I understand you represented Ben Abel."

"Yes, I did. Mr. Abel was a nuclear physicist and, as you can imagine, intimidated even me."

Mac smiles and said, "I've heard you might help me in my search for Bobby Livingston. I am working for his half-brothers."

"Yes, I might be able to help," said Katz.

"What do you remember about Bobby?" Mac asked as he sipped his tea.

"Bobby was the son of two research scientists who worked under my client. The scientists were Albert Livingston and Joline Hall. Albert was married, but Joline was not. Joline apparently gave up her parental rights to the child to Albert, and the child lived with the Livingstons for his first three or four years."

Mac said, "What happened to Bobby then?"

"Abel, who did not have any children, wanted Bobby and somehow talked the Livingstons into letting them adopt him."

Mac, so surprised he almost spilled his tea, said, "How? The boy was three or four years old. Why would the Livingstons give him up?"

Katz leaned forward and said, "Keep in mind Bobby was from an illegal union. Bobby was the product of two scientists, both working under Ben Abel. One of the scientists did not want the baby and planned to have an abortion. The other scientist did not want the baby to be aborted.

"Abel told Albert if he wanted to continue working in the industry, he must let his wife and him adopt Bobby. Albert Livingston's whole identity was tied up in his work. Whenever he left the premises, he took his work with him. So, Albert's choice was between a baby he took only to save the baby's life and his own life and career. Albert did not want the child; he wanted the child to live. If Joline wanted the child, Albert would have been glad.

"Ingrid Livingston loved the boy, but he was not hers, and

she had Gary, who was hers. She, of course, did not have any say in the matter.

"As to why Ben Abel and his wife wanted Bobby, I'm not sure. They said it was because they had no children of their own, and Bobby was a very smart four-year-old. Perhaps Abel was jealous of Albert and wanted what was his or at least did not want Albert to have it.

"I handled the adoption, and even I'm not sure why he was given up and why he was adopted," Art said as he shrugged his shoulders and held his hands out wide.

"Ben Abel died about ten years after he adopted Bobby. I do not know what happened to Bobby then. Abel's wife died the year before. By that time, I no longer represented Mr. Abel, so my knowledge ends there. I have no idea what happened to Bobby upon Ben's death. That's all I can tell you."

"Thank you for sharing with me. You have brought us closer to finding Bobby than we have been. Oh, do you know if Mr. and Mrs. Abel kept Bobby's name?"

"I'm not sure."

Alan thinks of Emory Walker and weeps. He had not discerned the depth of the young man's anguish and had not kept up with him to encourage and help him. Alan believes the mission of the church is to love, not condemn, anyone who has lost his way, and to show them the answer is in Christ alone. Maybe he is being called to do more.

"Hi, I'm Alan Livingston. I knew your son and wondered if we can meet so I can talk with you."

Mr. Walker answered, "You have some nerve calling us, Livingston. You are one of the reasons our son took his life, and you want to talk about it!"

"I want to ask you to forgive me."

"We will never forgive you, preacher, for what you did to our son. You had better not be calling here anymore if you value your life."

Walker slams the phone down; Alan drops his head and does not move for a long time.

Randy said, "Brother Alan, the last time you visited, I wanted to accept Jesus, but I was so tired I didn't think I could. A few days later, I was feeling better, so I got out my old Bible and read the verses you recommended. Before I even read all of them, I felt the Spirit urging me, so I gave my life to the Lord right then and there."

"You bless my soul, brother Randy. I will continue to pray for you. How are you feeling?"

"Like I don't have many days left, but I now have peace to know when I leave here, I'll be with my Jesus."

"Amen. I will see you again soon. Shall we pray together?"

After visiting, Alan heads for the compound. Randy is a bright light in an otherwise dark day. He had forgotten Riley is at the circus with Beth and Honcho, but it gives him time to relax after a busy day and to pray for the Walkers and others.

Soon after Alan arrives, Gary saunters in and says, "I've got some news. Our suspect, Roger Cutlow, was bound over for trial, the judge denying his motion to dismiss. Strange though, Alan, Roger wants to talk to you. I told him you can come by the jail tomorrow around eleven o'clock. Will that work?"

Alan said, "Yeah. I wonder why he wants to talk to me."

"Maybe he wants to apologize," said Honcho, who enters the room while they are talking.

"It's not every day I get to talk with a bona fide criminal, at least not one in jail. We know he is guilty. I trust Larry, and he said Roger is the one who got the orders from the boss."

"You will be under protection at the jail."

"God is our protector. He knows what is in someone's heart even before they do. Amazing God, isn't he!"

"Yes, he is," said Gary, as Riley came bounding in with Esther right behind him.

"How about it, Riley? Did you have fun?"

"Yes, I did. It was great! Then when I got home, Uncle Manny and Aunt Esther let me help them get ready for the yard sale at the fire station."

"You're a busy boy. You go wash up for supper, and I will be right behind you. What are we having, ladies?"

"We are visiting New Orleans tonight. We have gumbo, shrimp po-boys, a Caesar salad, and bread pudding."

"Wow, sounds great!"

"Well, I can't take much credit. Esther fixed almost everything while I was with Riley and Honcho at the circus."

After dinner, Alan and Riley go for a walk. Honcho goes too, a few steps behind. Riley talks about his play group and jumps up and down along with the puppies. He is excited to be going into the second grade.

"That is great, Riley. I am glad you are looking forward to school. We believe your momma will be home by then."

"I miss Momma so much," Riley said as he reached for Alan's hand. "Sometimes I cry myself to sleep. I love you, Daddy, and I love Momma too. Do you think God will let her come home?"

"Yes, I think God will bring her home to us. We will have a big party with balloons and cake and ice cream to welcome her home. You can show her how much you have learned from Aunt Beth and Manny. Maybe we will go fishing and put the fish in the freezer to have when she gets home. She loves fish and hushpuppies."

"I like fish and puppies too.

"Daddy, all the other kids have televisions, and they go to the movies. Why don't we?"

"We'll talk about it with Momma when she gets home."

When they return from their walk, Alan said, "I know you like to draw, Riley. If you draw a nice picture for Momma, when she gets home, she can put it on the refrigerator to look at every time she opens the door."

"Okay. I will do that right now. Can I draw and color in here?"

"Yes, you may draw and color in here. I don't know if you can."

"Well can I, or can't I?"

"Go get your crayons. I should leave teaching English to the English teachers. I'm not good at it."

"Okay. I'll be right back."

CHAPTER 23

"Brother Livingston, I'm Roger Cutlow."

"Hello, Roger."

Roger, handcuffed, sits stiffly at a table in the small interview room. His lawyer sits on the same side, and Alan sits across from them. Roger said, "I know you probably wonder why I wanted to see you. It goes back a few years. I guess you had just started preaching. I came in the back of a church, and you yelled at me. You told me the church was not open until some other time. I should come back then, and get my hair cut and put on some clean clothes before I came back."

Alan's mouth opens, and his eyes get wide. He vaguely remembers the encounter. Why he was so insensitive then, he did not know.

Roger continues, "I never went back to that church or to any other church. I was so humiliated. You really hurt my feelings. I did not have any clean clothes or any money for a haircut. I held onto the hurt until it turned into anger. I was angry for a long time, and then the anger became outright hate …"

"Excuse me, Roger. Brother Livingston, I need to speak with my client privately. If you will step outside for a minute."

"Certainly," said Alan as he gets up and leaves the room.

Mr. Wells sits back down and faces Roger, who said,

"I've decided to plead guilty, and I want to confess to Brother Livingston."

"Roger, have you thought this through? Are you sure you want to plead guilty? You know you are facing years in prison."

"Yes, I know, and yes, I want to plead guilty."

Alan returns, and Roger said, "Brother Livingston, while I was in jail this past month, some men came and brought us Bibles and taught us about Jesus. To make a long story short, I decided to follow Jesus and to ask him to help me change my life. I wanted to meet with you today to let you know that I no longer hold anything against you like I did."

"Roger, I am sorry I acted so horribly toward you. To think if it had not been for those men visiting the jail, you might have missed Jesus altogether, and it would have been all my fault. Please forgive me if you can."

"Well, that's what I meant to say. I forgive you. I have no choice but to forgive you. Jesus has forgiven me, and I am supposed to forgive others. I learned if I do not forgive others, God will not forgive me. I just wanted you to know.

"To be completely fair, though, I need to ask you to forgive me. I was involved in your wife's kidnapping. I do not know who was pulling the strings or how he knew I hated you, but he recruited me.

"Jim Boren and I did the actual kidnapping. Jim hates all preachers. I am talking to him and praying he will come to know Jesus. Larry has already given his heart to the Lord, and he wasn't involved in any of the crimes anyway."

Alan's heart skips a few beats as he brings his fist down on the table. Mr. Wells moves back out of his reach. Alan said through clenched teeth, "Roger, do you have any idea how it makes me feel to know you participated in forcibly taking my wife? It makes me want to hurt you. It makes me want to ruin your life. But then I would not be a good Christian if I do not forgive you, so I will, but those feelings are raw, and they probably will not go away for a long time. Have you ever been married? Do you have any idea how horrible it is to have someone you love taken violently from you? Do you know where they are holding my wife?"

Roger said, "Jim and I delivered her to a woman's house. I think she was going to take care of your wife.

"I am sorry I was involved. I let hate fester all that time, so I was easily talked into helping the kidnapper. I do not know what his issue is. He calls the shots and insists on perfection."

Mr. Wells said, "The police will check the place out. Do you know the address?"

"No, but I can lead the police to it."

"Do you know who else is helping the kidnapper?"

"No, Brother Livingston, I don't know them or anyone else besides Jim Boren and Larry Reed, but I know there are others."

"I appreciate your honesty. I know you did not have to confess, and I know you have been changed by our Lord Jesus Christ. If there is any way you can help me find my wife, if you think of anything at all, you know I will appreciate your help."

"If you don't mind, would you please pray for me?"

After Roger is taken back to his cell, Alan goes to Gary's office and sits down with a big sigh. Gary watched the interview and wants to ask Roger more questions. Alan said, "I can't believe Roger and Jim Boren took Anna from our home to that lady's house, blindfolded and bound. Anna must have been scared to death."

Gary said, "It was good Roger opened up to you. He was forthcoming only because he was saved in jail. I have got to find that group of men and thank them for visiting the jail and witnessing to the inmates. I wonder if Jim Boren and Jeff Hanson will get saved. We will keep praying. So far, we have seen God save Larry, Larry's father, Jason, and Roger."

"You're right," said Alan. "God's on the move; this case has the beginnings of a revival!"

Gary calls Milton and sets up a time to check out the place where Roger and Jim took Anna.

"How about lunch, Alan? Milton can't join us until this evening."

Once they reach the restaurant, fill their plates at the buffet, and pray, Alan gets the attention of a waitress and asks her for sweet tea. He then leans toward Gary and in a quiet, intense voice says, "Gary, I've got a confession to make. When the house burned down after Anna had been taken and a few times since, I have wanted to drink so badly that I sometimes think I cannot go on without a drink. But so far I've managed to stay away from the stuff."

Gary said, "I'm glad you haven't given in, Alan. Your struggle with alcohol never leaves you, does it?"

"No. I thought I had been completely delivered, Gary, and I believe I had, but the desire came back with a vengeance. It was strong and seemed justified under the circumstances. I had the good sense—or, more likely, God encouraged me—to call my sponsor from years ago. He must have been waiting for me to call. He and I talked for about two hours, and we prayed together. The next day, I went to Meridian to see him. He lives on a farm just out of town. We walked down the corn rows, across the pastures, and through the forests and talked for several hours.

"I was fine then until the accusations came down, and though I prayed and encouraged everyone, the demon drink still called to me. I was so close to giving in, but God intervened again through an unlikely source, Pete Boland! To God be the glory!"

"Amen. Brother, you could have come to me. I would have tried to help."

"I would have, Gary, if not for my pride and shame. You're always there for me, brother, and I thank God for you."

Gary asks Mac to investigate the law firm of Dillon Dubois. Mac is surprised by the request. "Dillon Dubois is familiar to me," said Mac, " because the lawyer helped me in a case involving the kidnapping of the son of a lawyer by the lawyer's son from a prior marriage. The son did not make it, and the lawyer was so heartbroken he committed suicide. I don't like to remember the case, but Dillon was a big help to me."

Gary said, "I just don't want to leave any stone unturned, no matter how small. Remember it was his or his firm's vehicle Larry was driving, and an attorney from his firm represents Jim Boren."

"Anna, the boss wants to see you pronto."

"Oh, Maria, maybe today is the day of his salvation."

"Here's the man with the blindfold."

"Hello, ma'am. Please come with me."

"Hello, Anna. I am sorry I have put you through this ordeal.

"As you know, God has been working on my heart, and I am almost persuaded to ask for his forgiveness.

"What caused me to consider God at all was listening to you witness to Maria. I have read the Bible, and I can tell you are a Christian by your love even for me, your kidnapper. I hope someday I will have the faith and love you have."

On the way to Southaven to locate the house where Anna had been taken, Gary asked Roger, "Do you know Donny Aldridge?"

"Yes, why?" said Roger.

"Was he involved in the kidnapping?" asked Gary.

"I don't know. I never saw him or heard from him. But the way he hated Alan and always wanted to get back at him, I will not be surprised if he is the kidnapper," said Roger.

Gary and Milton read the results of Donny's polygraph test. According to the examiner, Donny was most likely lying when he denied kidnapping Anna. Taken together with Roger's and others' assessment of Donny, it made him a credible candidate for the kidnapper. Yet there was no direct evidence of his actions.

Gary questions Charles Winters at Charles's home, saying, "Charles, have you decided to tell the truth about working with Jason Stone?"

"I have told you and Alan the absolute truth."

"How about your involvement with the security guard, Ricky Rivers?"

"I had no such involvement. I don't even know a Ricky Rivers!"

"Do you know Donny Aldridge?"

"No."

"You're sure?"

And the interview continues in that vein until Gary says, "You are coming with me, Charles. You are under arrest for assault and conspiracy to kidnap."

Next, Gary finds Arthur Loden at Jason's place of employment. He said, "Arthur, I need you to come to the station with me to answer some questions. Don't worry; your friend Charles will be there too."

Arthur breaks into a run, but Gary easily catches him, handcuffs him, and leads him to his car. Once at the station, Gary asked, "Do you know Donny Aldridge?"

"Yes, I know him, but I haven't seen him in a long time. What about it?"

"Didn't you and Donny get together for the kidnapping?"

"I am not going to answer any more questions. I want a lawyer."

Soon after the interview with Charles, Gary receives a call from Jason, who said, "They will kill me. They'll know I gave them up!"

"Calm down, Jason. Each of them will think the other one gave him up, and they are spending tonight in the jail. It is unlikely they will do anything to make them look more guilty than they already are."

"I'm afraid the boss will take action against me because I took two of his men out. Can I call you if anything looks suspicious?"

"Of course. I answer my phone night and day, and I want you to call if anything seems out of the ordinary."

Mac drops in to see Gary and said, "Remember I talked with Art Katz, Ben Abel's lawyer. After that conversation, I felt like I was at a dead end. Then, most likely in answer to prayer, I found a relative of Ben Abel. His name is Joseph Abel; he was Ben's brother; and he lives at the Veteran's Home in Jackson.

"I want to interview Joseph like yesterday, but I will have to wait until I find someone to stay with my wife. My daughter cannot this time. I will let you know as soon as I find someone. I feel good about this source. Maybe we'll find Bobby yet!"

"Okay, great! Let me know. Oh, did you find anything out about Dillon Dubois?"

"Yes, Dubois is single and an atheist but is considered a pillar of the community. He is on the Ethics Committee of the Bar Association and has a reputation of being honest and trustworthy.

"His college degree is from Harvard in biomedical engineering, and he has a law degree from Yale. He started his own law firm, which now has twelve lawyers and fifteen paralegals. The clientele is mostly small corporations and individuals. Most are civil cases, but there are a few criminal cases to keep things interesting.

"I understand the reason we are interested in Dubois is because he is the boss of Daniel Marks, who represents defendant Jim Boren, and because he or the firm owned one of the vehicles in the case. There is no evidence of any wrongdoing, only connections. Am I right?"

Joseph Abel greets Mac with a smile. He is in a wheelchair, and his room is neat and clean. Joseph said, "I remember Bobby when he first came to live with my brother. They were so excited to have him as their son. He was a young boy at the time."

"Do you know what happened to him when Ben died, and Bobby was fourteen?"

"No, but not from a lack of looking. I was in the air force. I never heard my brother or his wife mention what would happen to Bobby when they died. When I came home, I expected to see Bobby with one of our relatives, but he was nowhere to be found. I searched for him for months, with no success. I tried to find Ben's in-laws but did not find many of them, and the ones I found knew nothing.

"I got his lawyer to let me look through Ben's papers, and it was odd to me they made no reference to a guardian for Bobby. Of course, Ben was secretive.

"When I got your call, I was hoping you had found him."

"I'm sorry. I have been trying. His brothers are eager to meet him. Do you have any theories of what might have happened to him?"

"No. He just disappeared, leaving no clues. I do not know what happened. I just hope he has a good life."

"Any other clues you can give us?"

"No, I checked all of them out myself. No—wait a minute.

There was one piece of information I never ran down, a family who left for an extended stay in Europe about the same time Ben died and Bobby disappeared. They were close to my brother. I'll have to search for the name of the family."

"How long do you think it will take you to find it?"

"Oh, I don't know. Not too long."

"Will you call me as soon as you find it?"

"Yes, of course. I want to find Bobby too!"

CHAPTER 24

The boss sends for Anna and says, "I'm going away. You will be reunited with your family."

Anna says "Thank you! Wow! God is so good! This is amazing! But what about Maria?"

"I'll take her with me."

"But what about Jesus? You seem so close to salvation, but close is not good enough. You've got to make a commitment."

"Anna, I can't thank you enough for telling me about Jesus and for caring enough about me to forgive me."

"God loves you, boss, and to him you are precious. I pray you will surrender your life to Jesus and seek God's will sooner rather than later."

The kidnapper arranges for Maria to go to Cuba. He takes her to the airport and gives her money. He then tells his assistant, "Call Roy and tell him you are bringing a young woman to the bar in his motel. He is to watch out for her and to call this number.

"You get her there. Then join Maria at the airport. She has your ticket. You have to be there two hours before the flight. I do not know if I will be joining you. Do not worry. If I am caught, I will never give you up. Thank you for your faithful service. Here's some money, and you have your bank account."

"Thanks, boss."

Once the reunion of his victim and her family and the escape of his employees are ongoing, the kidnapper ponders his own future. Can he manage to keep up the ruse, or will he also have to run?

Gary goes to a hotel in Southaven to meet someone the owner called him about. He does not know who it is. When he sees her, he cannot believe his eyes! Can it really be Anna? Yes, praise the Lord!

Anna runs to Gary, and they grab each other in a big hug. Anna is laughing and crying at the same time, "Oh, Gary, words can't express how thankful I am!"

"Are you all right? Do you need to go see a doctor?"

"I'm fine. I am better than fine! I am free and on my way home! I will need to see a doctor soon but not today. Is Alan at the church or at home? And Riley?"

"I will call Alan and find out. Do you want me to tell him you are here or let it be a surprise when he sees you?"

"Let it be a surprise. Take me home, please."

"Actually, Alan and Riley and Beth and I are all living at the compound. Not long after you were kidnapped, your home was burned. We all moved to the compound for our safety."

"Who burned our home?"

"We believe it was the kidnapper."

"Are you sure?"

"Not 100 percent but pretty close."

"He never said anything about it. I cannot believe my home is gone! Oh, God, thank you for taking such good care of my family and me. My home gone. Oh, Lord, it hurts."

"We are so sorry about all that has happened to you, and I am thankful you are back."

"Thanks, Gary. I'm just going to rest while you drive."

———∞———

Gary said, "I'm home, and I brought a guest for dinner. Alan, where are you?"

"In here, Gary. I'm trying to get Riley to let me win a chess game!"

"Here's my guest," said Gary as he opens the door to the library and Anna walks in.

There is a moment of silence followed by screams of excitement and tears while they all hug and kiss and dance around in a circle.

"Anna," said Alan, "you're home! Praise the Lord! I have been praying for this reunion with all my heart! I never doubted God would bring you home to us in his time. How are you? Are you well?"

"Yes, Alan, I am well. Did you know we are going to have a baby? I will need to see a doctor soon, not that there are any problems but just as a matter of good prenatal care. I am so, so glad to be home with you and Riley."

"Momma, I've been praying for you. I go play with other kids now and have a great time. Aunt Beth is teaching me to play the piano. Uncle Manny and I have been working in the barn and in the garden, and we have puppies."

"Wow, Riley, you've grown so much since I left, and you've been so busy. You are a big boy now!"

"Yes, Momma. I'll be in second grade!"

"Wow," said Anna, hugging Riley and Alan again. "I love you guys so much!"

"Beth, how good to see you," said Anna, drawing Beth into a hug.

Beth said, "Not nearly as good as it is for me to see you!"

Alan said, "Here's Manny and Esther and Honcho. They are members of our family. Guys, this is my wife, Anna. Anna, these guys took good care of Riley and me while you were gone. I would not have made it without them and Gary and Beth."

"Thank all of you from the bottom of my heart," said Anna. "I am so happy to be here!"

Milton calls Gary and says, "We have the subpoena for Donny's electronics and bank account, but we cannot locate Donny. He seems to have dropped off the map."

Gary said, "That makes me wish I had agreed with you to arrest him when we had the chance. He may be gone for good."

Milton said, "I should have insisted."

"Have you issued an arrest warrant?"

"Yes."

"We should check the airlines in case he slipped out of the country."

Milton asked, "Have you talked with Anna yet about her knowledge of the kidnapper?"

Gary said, "Not yet. I am waiting until she spends a few hours with her family."

Milton said, "I understand, but part of me wants you to have interviewed her the moment you picked her up!"

The next day, Anna finds Beth in the laundry room and asks, "How did Alan do during my absence? I missed all of you so much."

"He was distraught and depressed, but he kept his head up around Riley. Riley missed you terribly, but he fared well. I took him to play with other kids, and he really enjoyed those playdates. Riley kept Alan sane. Without Riley, Alan would have crashed, quite possibly crawling back into a bottle. How about you, Anna? How were you treated?"

"The thing is, Beth, I was treated very well by my house guard. She was saved during our time together. The kidnapper scared me, but he treated me with respect. He never laid a hand on me."

"You are a blessed woman, Anna Meyer Livingston. Few, if any, kidnapping victims have been treated well."

"You're right, Beth, and the kidnapper was interested in Christianity, so we have at least one and possibly two additions to God's family from this ordeal."

Beth said, "That's not all. Several of the men accused of helping the kidnapper have put their faith in Jesus, so this situation is evidence of God's working all things together for good. I hope they catch the kidnapper! Don't you!"

Alan, Anna, and Riley go to Good News and listen to Joshua Strange. The church is packed. Word is out about Anna's return home from the kidnapper. Joshua calls them forward and asks if they want to say anything.so everyone can welcome Anna home and Alan back as the pastor of the church.

As soon as Alan and Anna come to the platform, the church rises, and the applause is deafening. Someone yells, "Hallelujah," and the choir starts singing and the church joins in. Anna is standing by Alan and tears are running down both their faces. She lifts her hand, and all is quiet.

"It is only because of God that I can stand before you today. Thank you so much for your prayers. I would not have made it through the ordeal without the Lord, and Alan would not have either. The woman who guarded me gave her life to Jesus, and the kidnapper asked me many questions about my faith and our Lord

Jesus Christ. I will not be surprised if he is saved and confesses his sins."

When Anna finishes speaking, Alan said, "If anyone needed proof that God exists, and God answers prayer, and God is good, and God saves! He is the great I AM! Come to the altar now and give your life to Jesus. You will be forever changed, and you will live forever. Do not wait. Come."

The altar is filled as the choir sings. Twenty-two people are saved, and many rededicate their lives. Josh and Alan minister to them. Revival is in the air.

Joel Benton comes to the platform and asks for everyone's attention. He says, "I want everyone to know our pastor never embezzled any money from this church. He is an honest man. I only made the accusation to save my grandson's life."

Next, Mary Jo Hinton comes to the platform and says, "Pastor Alan never made a pass at me. I was never in his office except when my husband was there too. I made my accusation against him to save the life of my sister."

Joshua and Alan minister to the newly saved, and Alan announces the church will have nightly revival services through Wednesday night or for as long as the Lord directs. There is much celebration; the people stay for almost three hours. Joshua and his wife and two children join Alan and all the family for a late lunch at the compound, and they continue celebrating. They agree this is a kidnapping revival. "Not only were many saved this morning, but several of the men who worked with the kidnapper have been saved, along with the kidnapper, most likely, and Anna's guard," says Alan.

Alan said, "Anna, do you think you will return to your nursing position?"

"I don't know yet, but I guess so," Anna said, reaching her hand out to touch his arm.

"I want you to take all the time you need to put this behind you," Alan said as he places his hand over Anna's.

"Thank you. I will."

Alan said, "I am reading your letters. It is wonderful you were so close to God during your captivity."

"Yes," said Anna. "God was close to me, and I was thrilled when Maria accepted Jesus and when the boss asked me about Christianity."

"God was with me too when I heard about the kidnapping, at the house fire, when I received the threatening notes, when the accusations were made, during the truck bombing and the many other events, all related to the kidnapping. I could never have made it through all those things without God.

"Did you get to know the kidnapper at all?"

"No. I just prayed for him and the other kidnappers to be saved, and I thanked God when the boss asked me about my salvation. I witnessed to him, and he said he listened to your sermons. He was always very respectful toward me. The only time he scared me was when he found out I was pregnant. He talked about, well, he talked about not letting me have your child. I told him I would die if he didn't let me have it," said Anna.

"Jon told me about Cliff, and I am so sorry that you went through such a horrible trauma, especially at such a young age," said Alan.

"Oh, Alan," Anna said as she wiped away her tears, "I'm sorry I didn't tell you. It just hurts my heart so much to think about it. I always planned to tell you. At least now you know."

"Yes, knowing about your experience explains some of your attitudes and fears. I love you so much, Anna. You have been through way more than most people. I want to protect you. In fact, I have beaten myself up about going to that church conference. But I know only God can protect you, and he has protected you and restored you to me. What an amazing God! What a wonderful wife!" Alan wraps Anna in a big hug and holds her tightly, both crying and knowing that more tears, healing tears, would come in the days ahead.

———∽∾∽———

Gary said, "Anna, let me know when you feel able to talk about your experience. The police need your help in catching and convicting the kidnapper and his associates."

"Gary, I can talk with you now. I would rather not go to the station. Will that be all right?"

"Yes, we will go into the security office so I can video the interview. We will start when you were abducted from your house."

After detailing the kidnapping from its inception, Anna answers questions about her captivity, including the house guard. Gary asked, "What is her name?"

"Her name is Maria."

"What about her last name?"

"I'll have to think on that."

"Were there other members of the kidnapper's team known to you?"

"He had an assistant who blindfolded me whenever I was taken to see the boss."

"Do you know his name?"

"No."

"So, you were blindfolded when you met the kidnapper. What about his voice? Would you recognize it again?"

"No. He used something that made his voice sound very strange."

"Is there anything you can tell us to help us find this kidnapper?"

"No, but don't you already have the two men who took me under arrest?"

"Yes, we arrested and convicted them, but we still need to arrest the one who called the shots, the real kidnapper."

"But why? Isn't it enough to have the ones who actually carried out the work?"

"Well, no. I understand the kidnapper was very well behaved around you."

"Yes, it's hard for me to think of him as the kidnapper because I prayed so much for him to receive Jesus as his Savior, and he was almost persuaded before my release."

Gary makes himself comfortable in Milton's office and says, "I don't think Anna wants us to catch the kidnapper."

"That's not so unusual," said Milton, playing with his pen. "There's a syndrome called the Helsinki syndrome or the Stockholm syndrome. Both refer to the psychological condition where a victim develops sympathetic feelings toward the kidnapper. You are too young to remember Patty Hearst, who was kidnapped by a terrorist. She identified with him so much that she committed crimes with him."

Gary said, "I've heard about the case and a couple of others. One factor here is how well Anna was treated by the house guard and the kidnapper. Spending twenty-four hours a day with someone for two months is plenty of time to develop a relationship. Another factor is Anna's Christian witness. She may believe the kidnapper will turn himself in once he surrenders to the Lord."

"What is done about a victim who has the syndrome?"

Milton said, "Psychological counseling is the only treatment I know about. Now Anna may or may not have this syndrome."

Gary said, "Should we mention it to Alan?"

Milton said, "We can tell him about the possibility and counsel him to be sensitive."

About six weeks later, Mac calls Gary and says, "Joseph Abel called this morning. The family who disappeared when Ben Abel died and Bobby disappeared, was the Dubois family."

"Dubois? I wondered if there is any relation to the lawyer, Dillon Dubois."

"I don't know, Gary, but it seems likely. Do you want to call him, or should I?"

"Since you know him, you call him."

A few minutes later, Mac called and said, "Dillon wants to meet with you and Alan and me. When are you available?"

"Hey, Milton," said Gary, his smile widening as he spoke. "We arrested Donny Aldridge."

"Great! I had about given up. Where did you find him?"

"Believe it or not, we found him at the hotel where we found Anna. It turns out the hotel bar is one of Donny's favorite watering holes."

"Has he said anything?"

"Just that he wants his lawyer."

"Good going, Gary. Keep me posted."

CHAPTER 25

Gary said, "Please have a seat, Dillon. Alan and Mac will be here any minute. Can I get you anything?"

"No, thank you."

When Mac and Alan arrive and everyone is seated, Dillon said, "My name was once Bobby Livingston. I'm your half-brother."

Alan and Gary jump up. Alan said, "I can't believe it!"

Gary said, "Wow! We only found out about having another brother recently. We read about you in Mother's diary."

Mac said, "I talked with your biological mother, Joline Hall; Ben's lawyer, Art Katz; some of Ben's neighbors; and Ben's brother, Joseph Abel. It was Joseph who gave us the Dubois name."

"This is amazing," said Alan. "We live in the same town, and I had no idea!" Alan turned to Mac and said, "We owe you big-time! Thank you so much for bringing us together."

Gary and Alan spoke at the same time. "Go ahead, Alan."

"Oh, I was just going to invite Dillon and Mac to dinner. How about it, guys?"

Dillon said, "Sure, I'd love to come."

Mac said, "I'd love to come too, but I'd better get home. Congratulations, everybody!"

"Wow," said Riley. "You're my Uncle Dillon? Now I have three uncles, you and Uncle Gary and Uncle Manny."

"Who's Manny?" Dillon asked.

Gary said, "He, along with his wife, Esther, have taken care of the compound since our parents' days. They remember you."

"Do you have a wife, Gary?"

"Yes." He yells, "Beth, honey, guess who's here."

"Oh, Gary, you're home."

"Beth, this is Dillon Dubois."

"Ah, the lawyer."

"Yes, but he is also Bobby, the brother you and Esther found in Mother's diary."

Beth's eyes get big. She smiles and extends her hand, then walks over and gives him a big hug, saying, "Welcome to the family!"

"Esther," Beth calls. Esther comes out of the kitchen with flour in her hair and on her apron, and says, "You didn't tell me we have company."

"It's Bobby, Esther. Can you believe it? Mac found Bobby whose name is Dillon Dubois."

"This is so amazing. I did not think we would ever find you, and here you are. Welcome!"

Riley said, "Let's go the barn so Uncle Dillon can meet Uncle Manny."

Alan drops in at Dillon's office and says, "Dillon, you are invited to come to our church."

"Thank you. I have been an atheist most of my life, following the Dubois family tradition, but I will come. My colleagues will be astounded. They've been working on me to go to church for a long time."

"Sam," Alan said, "I've got some news."

"Well, spill it, man. You're in the right place."

"Dillon Dubois is my half-brother."

"You're kidding!"

Alan tells Sam the story, and Sam suggests they print it in the family section of the newspaper.

Gary contacts Donny's lawyer, Susan Goldman, about meeting her client.

"My client is innocent, Detective Livingston, and will be glad to talk to you. He has nothing to hide. You have already spoken to him at length and have subjected him to a polygraph test. What more do you want to know?"

"As you know, he failed the polygraph test, and he will undoubtedly be indicted."

"Neither of those indicate guilt. The polygraph is not evidence, and everyone knows grand juries will indict on very slim evidence."

"What about all his prison buddies?"

"None of them identifies Donny as the kidnapper."

"That doesn't exonerate him, as none of the suspects has ever met the kidnapper face-to-face, and I understand he uses some kind of voice distorter."

"Let's wait for the grand jury before we meet."

"Alan," said Dillon, "I felt the words of your sermon in my heart, and my eyes were opened to your message. Without a doubt, you are a gifted preacher."

"Thank you, but God gets all the praise. I was an alcoholic until Jesus rescued me, cleaned me up, and turned me into his messenger. So, Dillon, maybe you would like to join our

Wednesday-night Bible study. But for now, you are coming to Sunday dinner, aren't you?"

"Wouldn't miss it for anything—best cooking in the state!"

At one Sunday meal, Anna and Dillon are left at the table. Dillon pushes away from the table and said, "Well, Anna, are you suffering any ill effects from your kidnapping experience?"

Anna said, "I don't have PTSD, if that's what you mean, probably because of my good relationship with the woman who guarded me. She took care of me, and I witnessed to her. She was saved before we parted. I miss her and pray for her every day. I also pray for the kidnapper."

"I pray for the Dubois family, as they are all atheists."

"So, are you a believer?" asked Anna.

"Probably not the way you mean, but I feel a burden to pray for my family," said Dillon.

"You are either a believer or a you are a nonbeliever. There is no in-between."

"Changing subjects," said Dillon, "I understand they arrested the kidnapper."

Anna quickly looks down and says quietly, "What's his name?"

"Donny Aldridge."

"Gary," said Anna, "Dillon tells me you've arrested the kidnapper. How did you find him?"

"He went to school with Alan, and he has an intense hatred for Alan. The reason for the hatred is that Alan 'stole' Donny's girlfriend in high school."

"That seems an unlikely motive for kidnapping."

"Yes and no. Emotions, especially strong emotions like hatred, can last years and grow stronger as the years go by. Donny has kept surveillance on Alan, you, and Riley."

"I would like to talk with him. I can probably tell you if he is the kidnapper from the content of our conversations."

"But I thought you didn't want us to catch the kidnapper."

The three brothers are playing a round of golf at the Tupelo country club. "So, Dillon, how did you find out we are brothers?" said Alan after teeing off.

"It's a long story, and I've known for a long time," said Dillon as he places his tee.

"Well," said Gary, "how did you find out?"

Dillon hits a long drive and says, "The Dubois family knew my family history and told me about you when I was home from law school."

Gary tees off and his ball slices, and he said, "So, why didn't you tell us years ago?"

"Like I said, it's a long story, and it would be better to talk about it in a more formal setting," said Dillon.

"Sounds serious," said Alan.

"Let's finish this game first since I seem to be winning."

CHAPTER 26

Mac joins Alan and Gary at the compound. They seat themselves around the table in the library and ask not to be disturbed. Dillon joins them, apologizing for being late.

"I have enjoyed the past weeks, and I will always hold this time together close to my heart."

"You sound like you are leaving or dying. You don't have a terminal illness, do you?" said Gary.

"Not a terminal illness, but in a way, it is terminal," says Dillon as he stands up and looks at each of them for a few moments. "I guess I should just get to it."

No one spoke.

"I have a confession to make," says Dillon, as he looks at the floor. "I held it against your parents, well, our parents, for giving me away when I was four years old. I nursed the hurt for many years. It grew from a hurt to an obsession. I wanted to hurt you, since our parents were no longer around for me to hurt them. I could not see beyond the pain. Hate filled my heart and soul, my very being.

"I chose you, Alan, to vent my rage against because you are a preacher, and I have had some bad experiences with preachers. The assault against your church by Jason Stone allowed me to express my animosity toward a Christian church, but mostly it was against you, Alan, as partial payment for my parents' crime. My plan was to torment you, Gary, when I finished with Alan."

Mac, Alan, and Gary sit with their mouths open, but no words are spoken. Finally, Gary says, "So, are you saying what I think you are saying? What about Donny Aldridge?"

"Yes, I'm turning myself in. I represented Donny a few years ago and learned of his feelings against Alan, and he knew others from prison who hated Alan too. When I planned the kidnapping and related attacks, Donny worked for me, though he did not know I am the kidnapper. He rounded up almost everyone who held a grudge against you, Alan, but I cannot let him take my punishment.

"More importantly, I have given my life to the Lord Jesus, thanks to the Lord, Anna's testimony and encouragement and Alan's preaching. I have lived with the hatred for years, and now I must pay the price for my horrific actions."

Anna slips into the room quietly while Dillon makes this pronouncement and says, "I didn't know it was you, Dillon, but I did know the 'boss' would turn himself in once he surrendered his life to the Lord. You've made the two best decisions of your life."

"I don't know what to say, Anna, except I am sorry. If I could do it all over again, knowing what I know now, I would have reached out for help and accepted Jesus. Please forgive me. I am so sorry."

"Dillon, you know I forgive you. It is hard though, real hard, especially for burning my home. Nevertheless, I must forgive you, or God won't forgive me."

Alan stands, staying as still as a statue for about two minutes, glaring, his face becoming red and sweaty, his hands curling into fists. He moves Anna back and gets right up in Dillon's face. When he speaks, his voice is low and menacing. He pokes his finger into Dillon's chest, saying, "You. You. You kidnapped Anna and kept her from me for over two months. You burned our home. You tried to destroy the church and my reputation. You threatened and tormented me. I would kill you if I could live with myself and be faithful to my God.

"No matter what was done to you, we did not do it; our parents did. It was years ago. Nothing done to you and nothing that could have been done to you gave you the right to take this woman away from me and our little boy. Nothing! Do you hear me? Nothing! She never did anything to hurt you; my son did not; my brother did not; and I did not. Nothing!

"How could you wreck our lives and burn our home? I am surprised you did not kill us. You were an atheist, so you probably would have if God had not intervened. Here I was so thankful for you, my brother, and find out you are slime, Dillon, absolute slime.

For a moment, no one dares to breathe.

The pressure in the room is suffocating.

"Alan, I know I am slime. I do not blame you for wanting to kill me. I deserve it. I know I hurt you, and Anna, and your little boy more than any human should have to endure."

"Dillon," said Alan, "I am called to forgive. I preach on it in some form almost every Sunday. In fact, I choose to forgive you, but it will take a long time, I think, for my feelings to change. Why did you wait until now to confess?"

"I wanted to experience having brothers and making memories to see me through the trials ahead. These past months have meant more to me than I can ever thank you enough for. I know I am selfish. I know being sorry for all I have done does not help, but I am deeply sorry and ashamed. Anna witnessed to me and led me to Jesus. I am no longer burdened with the hatred I felt toward our parents and you and Gary.

"When I plead guilty, I will be sentenced to many years in prison. I deserve whatever sentence I get and more. I may spend my life behind bars. I may die there.

"But the good news is I now belong to Jesus.

"And Jesus has set me free."

ABOUT THE AUTHOR

The author was adopted when she was three years old by a farmer and a schoolteacher. She became a lawyer, practicing in Washington, D.C., Houston, Texas; and the Mississippi Gulf Coast. She eventually returned home, experiencing spiritual renewal and birthing her only son, Nathan McIntosh, who is now a lawyer living in Jackson, Mississippi.

Printed in the United States
By Bookmasters